D1074265

Thirty-One Brothers and Sisters

The South African veld, with its gentle rolling hills and soft green meadows watered by many streams, is the background for this unusual story about Nomusa, daughter of a Zulu chief.

Nomusa is warmhearted and generous and affectionate; she loves all her little brothers and sisters and enjoys helping to care for them. But she is strong and brave and daring, too; she feels that girls' work is dull and boys' work is much more exciting, and much more fun.

More than anything else, Nomusa yearns to go with the men on the annual elephant hunt. But she knows this is impossible. As her mother says, "Girls never *go on elephant hunts!"*

After Nomusa's adventure with a fierce wild boar, her father, Chief Zitu, rewards her bravery. In a final climax, Nomusa realizes that being a girl has its own rewards.

A sympathetic, engrossing story about a primitive civilization of today. Nomusa is a heroine whom girls will envy and boys will admire.

REBA PAEFF MIRSKY

Thirty-One
Brothers and Sisters

Illustrations by W. T. Mars

FOLLETT PUBLISHING COMPANY · CHICAGO · NEW YORK

FIC
Mirsky

*Copyright © 1952, by Reba Paeff Mirsky. All rights reserved.
No part of this book may be reproduced in any form without
written permission from the publisher. Manufactured in the
United States of America. Published simultaneously in Canada
by The Ryerson Press, Toronto.*

Library of Congress Catalog Card Number: 52-13782

NINTH PRINTING

Follett Publishing Company
1010 West Washington Boulevard
Chicago, Illinois 60607

TL 8610

HUGH STEPHENS LIBRARY
STEPHENS COLLEGE
COLUMBIA, MISSOURI

800.33
M67th

*To the late John Dube of Ohlange
and my other Zulu friends*

112959

THE
Charles W. Follett Award

PRESENTED ANNUALLY
For Worthy Contributions to Children's Literature

JOHNNY TEXAS	*by Carol Hoff*	1950
ALL-OF-A-KIND FAMILY	*by Sydney Taylor*	1951
THIRTY-ONE BROTHERS AND SISTERS	*by Reba Paeff Mirsky*	1952
TORNADO JONES	*by Trella Lamson Dick*	1953
LITTLE WU AND THE WATERMELONS	*by Beatrice Liu*	1954
MINUTEMEN OF THE SEA	*by Tom Cluff*	1955
NO AWARD		1956
CHUCHO, THE BOY WITH THE GOOD NAME	*by Eula Mark Phillips*	1957
SOUTH TOWN	*by Lorenz Graham*	1958
MODEL A MULE	*by Robert Willis*	1959
"WHAT THEN, RAMAN?"	*by Shirley L. Arora*	1960
NO AWARD		1961
ME AND CALEB	*by Franklyn E. Meyer*	1962
NO AWARD		1963
ACROSS FIVE APRILS	*by Irene Hunt*	1964

Thirty-One Brothers and Sisters

ONE: # A Morning Adventure

Although it was morning, inside the straw hut it was still dark. Nomusa lay on her little bamboo mat, stretching and scratching her lean, naked body. She yawned and thought to herself:

Yo, I am still so sleepy! If only I did not have to get up to fetch water from the stream! Why must I leave my comfortable mat when Mdingi and Kangata may still sleep? Zulu boys have all the fun, and they don't work nearly so hard as the girls.

Nomusa rolled up her mat, moving quietly so as not to wake her baby sister and her little brother. They lay sleeping on a larger mat next to her mother, Makanya.

As Nomusa passed the iron pot, she picked out a piece of cold sweet potato to eat on the way to the stream. Taking a clay jar in one hand and holding the sweet potato in the other, she crawled out of the low opening of her hut.

Coming out from the darkness of the hut into the brilliant sunshine made Nomusa's eyes blink. She took a deep breath of the fresh air. What a wonderful day!

She stood for a moment looking about the kraal. There were six other huts in the enclosure, each shaped like a huge beehive. Five belonged to the five other wives of Nomusa's father. The sixth hut, which was the biggest, was where her father, Chief Zitu, lived. The seven huts were in a circle on a hillside overlooking a wide, lovely valley.

As Nomusa stood there she saw no sign of anyone stirring in the other huts. Usually she saw some of her half sisters, many of whom were about the same age as herself, crawling out of their huts to go for water too. It was more fun going together. But today Nomusa's father was coming to visit their hut, and everything had to be ready earlier than usual.

She left the kraal and walked quickly down the well-worn dirt path leading to a clear stream in the valley. As she hurried along, Nomusa looked toward one of the other hills to see if any smoke was coming from the kraal of their nearest neighbor. Yes, there was a thin wisp of smoke curling up from a hut. That meant some of them were already awake and cooking. Nomusa wondered if the smoke were coming from Damasi's hut. There was much work to be done in his kraal, too; for tomorrow all the children from Nomusa's kraal would go to a party in Damasi's.

For a moment Nomusa forgot she was in a hurry and stood there thinking as she chewed the last bit of sweet potato. She gazed dreamily into the soft green meadows of the valley, encircled by rolling hills and

watered by many little streams. It was the season after the heavy rains, and now the mimosa trees were covered with yellow blossoms and feathery green leaves. The thorn bushes looked softer with their new thick foliage. In some of the trees orchids, green and brown, clung to branches by their thick stems. The sandhills beyond, usually so bare, were now blanketed with grass and wild flowers so that one hardly knew there were jagged rocks beneath.

With the water jar on her left hip and her right arm hanging loosely by her side, Nomusa looked like an ebony statue, her body slim and strong, her hair a mass of short black curls covering her head. She looked as much like a boy as a girl. Her snub nose and smiling mouth were only a little different from those of her father's other children, but there was something special about her intelligent brown eyes.

Nomusa hurried to make up for stopping, and reached the swollen stream in the valley warm and out of breath. What if her father arrived in their hut before she returned with the water? What a disgrace that would be!

She began sloshing her jar back and forth in the stream to fill it. Much as she wanted to, she would not take time now for a dip in the water. Perhaps there would be time for a swim when she came for water again at noon.

No sound broke the morning calm except the gentle splashing and sloshing of the water as Nomusa pulled her jar from one side to another. Then a sudden screech coming from one of the trees overhanging the stream made Nomusa look up. Above her head she saw two parrots sitting side by side. Their brilliant feathers bristled stiffly, and they shifted uneasily on the branch. What was worrying them, she wondered?

The parrots flapped their wings, and again they screeched, this time more insistently. A long scarlet feather slowly fluttered to the ground, and Nomusa dashed out of the stream to catch it before it landed. She did not want it to get wet and bedraggled on the moist ground.

But it was not easy to clamber over the rocks and stones. The feather fell into the deep grass beneath the tree before she could catch it.

Just as she was about to grasp it, there was a shriek from the parrots and a loud hiss. Nomusa jumped back and almost fell into the stream as she stumbled against a tree stump. She jumped up on the stump and looked fearfully down into the grass to see what had hissed at her.

It was the imamba, one of the most dreaded snakes. Its body was a bright flame color; as she watched, the creature raised its head from the ground and spread out the brilliant skin on its neck so that it looked as if it had a hood.

The imamba turned toward Nomusa and hissed again. Nomusa knew that this meant the snake was about to strike. She could see its short fangs, its back-curved teeth. Its lidless eyes were round and cold and cruel.

Nomusa broke into a cold sweat as she saw the snake's long, slender tongue, forked at the end, waving like an antenna to detect the odors and vibrations in the air. The imamba was looking for her so that when he spat his poison at her he would make a direct hit. She knew just how he would do it.

He would throw his body forward, and two jets of his venom would shoot out from the ends of his fangs. If this poison reached so much as scratch on her skin, it could kill her. If it got into her eyes, it would blind her, perhaps forever.

There was a large stone nearby, but Nomusa knew that her people never killed snakes, no matter how

dangerous they were. Snakes were full of evil spirits that would avenge themselves on the killer.

Nomusa wanted to run, but she knew better. Instead, she stood without the slightest movement, so as to keep the snake from striking. The imamba swayed his head slightly in a rhythmical motion that made Nomusa almost dizzy as she watched.

How long, she wondered, would they remain staring at each other before something happened? If she made the least move now, the imamba would surely strike. A few drops of sweat oozed down her nose and made the tip of it itchy, but Nomusa dared not lift a finger to scratch it.

The parrots had now grown unusually still, as if they were watching the outcome of the contest. Why did they no longer shriek or screech? All at once there was a swift blur of an object that flew to one side of the imamba, causing the snake to turn quickly in that direction.

Nomusa made a mighty spring from the stump, landing in the stream with such a noisy splash that the water rose over her in foaming bubbles.

She was safe!

TWO: # A House with One Room

When she returned with the water,
Nomusa saw her little brother Themba rolling in the
dust in front of their hut. His chubby body was covered
with dirt, and he looked like a brown gingerbread boy
covered with gray powdered sugar.

"What a story I have for you, Themba!"

But Themba spied the water jar. "I want a drink.
Give me a drink! Give me a drink, Nomusa!"

Nomusa brought the edge of the water jar to her
small brother's eager lips. Water ran down his chin and
over his fat body as he drank noisily.

Nomusa's dog, Puleng, came running out of the

hut. He showed his happiness at seeing Nomusa by running around her in crazy circles.

"Thirsty, Puleng?" Nomusa cupped her hand and poured some water into it for the dog to drink.

Just then Nomusa heard a voice behind her.

"*Sakubona,* Nomusa!"

It was her half sister, Sisiwe, who lived in the hut next to Nomusa's. They had the same father but not the same mother.

"What is the story, Nomusa?" Themba broke in eagerly. If his sisters began talking, he might never hear it.

"Well," Nomusa began, showing them the beautiful red and green feather, "it all began with this."

Sisiwe exclaimed over the parrot feather, but Themba clamored for the story.

Nomusa described her encounter with the imamba with lively words and gestures. Her audience was much impressed.

"And you went back for the feather!" said Sisiwe. "I should never have dared.

"You are lucky to have escaped—and to have the

beautiful feather," Sisiwe said, touching it admiringly.

"I have something else," added Nomusa. She opened the little deerskin bag that hung about her neck. This bag was her only pocket, and into it went all Nomusa's small treasures.

She took out a golden-yellow pebble, smooth and round, about the size of her thumbnail.

"How lovely!" Sisiwe exclaimed. "Where did you get it?"

"I found it on the ground as I returned from the stream."

"The most exciting things always happen to you, Nomusa," Sisiwe said. "How did you happen to be so early today?"

"I am early because our father is coming to visit us today, Sisiwe."

"He visited our hut yesterday. He wore a new belt of wildcat tails and looked very handsome," Sisiwe said proudly.

Nomusa was very proud of their father, too. Zitu was one of the most powerful Zulu chiefs, and head of the Zulu king's council. He was rich, rich enough to

have six wives, and this was why Nomusa was lucky
enough to have thirty brothers and sisters.

"I heard our father talking to my mother about
the elephant hunt," Sisiwe went on. "This time he is
taking some of our older brothers with him."

Nomusa's brown eyes grew big with excitement.
"Oh, Sisiwe, how I should love to go! Do you suppose I
could?"

Sisiwe opened her eyes in astonishment. "A girl
go on an elephant hunt? Who ever heard of such a
thing? Why, Nomusa, you talk as if you were our
brother Mdingi!"

"It is true that I do not like girls' work," Nomusa
said sadly.

"Nomusa!" Makanya called out sharply from within the hut.

"I am here, my mother," answered Nomusa, quickly crawling through the low opening of the hut. A
delicious smell of food cooking enveloped her as she
entered. Corn mush and bananas were steaming in a
pot over the fire.

After the dazzling sunshine outdoors, it took one's

eyes several seconds to be able to see inside the dark hut. It was just one large room; on the long pole extending from one end of the hut to the other hung baskets, wooden milk pails, gourds, and other things used in the vegetable gardens.

There was a saucerlike hole in the middle of the floor. Here they made the fire for cooking. Nomusa and her mother had gone to great trouble to pound a mixture of ant-heap sand, clay, and cow dung into the dirt floor, pounding and rubbing it with large smooth stones so it would gleam and glisten. She hoped her father would notice that they were good housekeepers.

"What kept you so long, my daughter?" asked Makanya. "I have been waiting for the water. Did you forget your father is coming to visit us? Stir the fire while I feed Bala."

Nomusa's mother gently laid the baby on a mat while she took an earthenware jar from the cool earth on one side of the room. In this jar was milk that had been left to sour into thick, large clots. The milk was cold and curdlike. Then Makanya picked up Bala and held her on her grass-skirted lap. The fat baby began to coo expectantly, holding up her brown, dimpled hands to her mother. Like a bird she opened her mouth, uttering cooing sounds. Makanya slowly poured some of the clotted milk into the baby's mouth. Bala began to smack her lips happily, but suddenly her expression turned into one of disappointment and disgust. She did not like her new food, and she would not swallow it, but began spitting it out as fast as she could. The clotted milk dribbled over her chin and down her chubby body.

But the thick sour clots were good for babies, and Nomusa's mother was determined that Bala should swallow them. She tried again to pour some of the nourishing clotted milk into the baby's mouth. This time Bala held her lips tightly closed.

Looking on anxiously, Nomusa thought it a pity that the baby did not yet have sense enough to know how good clotted milk tasted. She and her brothers loved it and did not get it half often enough.

"Nomusa!" called her mother. "Hold Bala's arms."

"Oh, Mother, I do not like to do this," said Nomusa. She was always unhappy when her little sister cried.

Makanya pinched together Bala's nostrils so that

she could not breathe. At once the baby opened her mouth for air, and when she did so, her mother quickly poured in some of the clotted milk. Bala choked and spluttered, but finally she had to swallow what was in her mouth. Frantically she struggled, and tiny as she was, she showed a strength that grew out of terror and desperation. She let out a fierce cry of rage which almost brought tears to Nomusa's sorrowful eyes.

"Yo, I am glad that's over," said Nomusa.

By this time Bala was covered with white splashes, and some of the clots had fallen on her mother's skirt.

"Here, Puleng!" called Nomusa.

Into the hut he came running, followed by Themba, who was not yet tall enough to have to crawl in through the low entrance of the hut, but did it to imitate the older children and to show he was grown up.

The dog did not have to be told what he had been called for. Without delay, he began licking off the milk splashes from Bala's naked little body, leaving her skin smooth and moist. The baby seemed to enjoy the dog's warm tongue on her body. It soothed her and made her forget how miserable she had been.

"Now the water, Nomusa," said her mother.

Nomusa brought it to her. Her mother took a large mouthful of the water, held it in her mouth a little until it was warm, and then squirted it on Bala. She did this over and over again until the delighted baby was thoroughly washed. She was then laid on her mother's mat, where she promptly stuck two fingers in her mouth and fell asleep.

Seeing that the clotted milk jar had not been put away, Themba begged softly, "I'm hungry, Nomusa. Me, too."

Nomusa poured some of the milk into his mouth.

"Here, little greedy. But then you must let me wash you."

She filled a hollow gourd with water and held it high over Themba's head, letting the water trickle over him. Themba danced up and down holding his hands over his head and shouting, "It's raining, it's raining!"

"*Tula!*" warned his mother. "You'll wake the baby."

Nomusa began rubbing her hand up and down his sturdy little body to clean him. She loved all her little sisters and brothers, even those belonging to Zitu's other wives.

"I'm going to eat now, Themba. Run outdoors. When I have finished and done some work for mother, I'll come and play *Hlungulu* with you."

This was Themba's favorite game; so he ran out of the hut, forgetting in his haste that he should have crawled out if he was to be thought grown up.

THREE: # A Visit from the Chief

Nomusa took up a little grass basket into which she put some of the food cooking in the pot.

She picked out pieces of corn and banana, putting them into her mouth and sucking the juice from her fingers with great relish.

As she ate, she watched her mother getting ready for her husband's visit. Makanya was busily greasing her body so she would look clean and shiny.

She rubbed her arms, then her legs, then her whole body, with fresh, sweet-smelling butter. It had been made the day before from cream from Makanya's own cows.

"Nomusa, when you have finished eating, I should like you to help me comb my hair."

"I have finished now, my mother."

"Then here are the porcupine quill and the comb."

The comb was a wooden one which Makanya had made herself. "Remember to comb my hair straight up into a peak," she said. "Some day when you are married you will wear your hair the same way."

Nomusa combed her mother's short, thick hair up from the back of her neck, shaping and slanting it backward from her forehead. To look proper, the hair had to end in a peak just back of the top of her head.

Every little while Nomusa had to rub grease into the hair so that it would stand up stiffly and stay in shape. With the porcupine quill she picked at the hair to keep the strands in place. It took patience and much combing and greasing to make the hair stay where it was supposed to.

After a while, Makanya carefully ran her hand over her head to feel the shape of her hair.

"Well done, my daughter," she said.

"What skirt will you wear today?" asked Nomusa.

"I shall wear the new oxhide one," said Makanya.

"Oh, you will look beautiful!"

Nomusa knew it was only a very special occasion that would induce her mother to wear the oxhide skin instead of her short grass skirt. For days and days she had watched her mother water-soak the skin, which had come from one of her own cattle. When it was soft, she had helped her mother pull out all the hairs. It had been long and tedious work. After that, they had both used sharp thorns and scratched and scratched at one side of the skin until it was as soft as a baby's ear.

Part of the skin became a skirt, part was used for Nomusa's best neck-pocket. Another part was used as a sling in which her mother carried the baby when she was working in the vegetable garden. The rest of the skin was saved until it should be needed.

Finally Makanya took from the rafters of the hut some bead bracelets and a necklace she kept hidden there. These she put on while Nomusa stood to one side, marveling at her mother's beauty. Makanya was tall and well-shaped. Her muscles were firm and strong. When she laughed, her white teeth glistened, making her smooth skin look darker still. No wonder Nomusa's father had had to give ten cows in order to get her

mother as a wife. She had heard that none of his other
wives had cost that much.

"You are beautiful, my mother!" exclaimed
Nomusa admiringly.

Just then they heard the sound of a man clearing
his throat in front of the entrance to the hut.

"He is here!" said Makanya excitedly, a slight pink
color appearing under her skin.

The small amount of daylight which came into
the hut through the entrance was blocked as a large
figure came crawling in.

"*Sakubona,*" Zitu greeted them, smiling. The Zulu
chief was magnificent in a belt of wildcat tails and a
necklace of blue beads around his neck.

"*Usaphila,*" answered Nomusa and her mother.

Always a little shy with her father, Nomusa partly
hid behind her mother.

Makanya said, "Nomusa, get your father's mat."

Nomusa got out the new bamboo mat her mother
had made especially for him and unrolled it on the
smooth floor. On this Zitu squatted. He took out of his
belt the horn of an ox and some tobacco. After stuffing

the horn with the tobacco, he took an ember from the fire and lit his pipe. Silently he began smoking.

Nomusa's mother now brought out all the good things she had made for her husband to eat. On a large grass plate she put chicken, pumpkin, yams, mealies, roast bananas. Then she brought beer. On Zitu's lap Makanya placed some tobacco she had grown especially for him.

At first, Nomusa's father pretended to be indifferent to the food, but the tantalizing smells proved too much for him. He laid down his oxhorn pipe and began eating with great gusto. He ate noisily, smacking his lips and belching from time to time. Nomusa and her mother did not utter a word while he was eating. They sat quietly, moving only when they had to take away his empty plate and fill it again. The Zulu chief ate and ate. Nomusa wondered how he could eat so much. From time to time an extra loud belch came out of him. Then Nomusa and her mother exchanged happy glances. They heard and saw that Zitu was enjoying their food.

Finally he licked his fingers thoroughly, showing

he had finished. He looked at Nomusa and her mother smilingly. That was all, but it was enough to make them feel repaid for all the effort they had gone to in order to please him.

Zitu sat on his mat, a strong handsome figure. His

muscular legs looked as though they could walk forty miles a day easily. Nomusa had heard that he often walked that much when he was out on a hunt. She wondered, as she kept her shining eyes on her father, whether he would say something about the elephant hunt. She waited and hoped.

Suddenly the chief spoke, pointing to the sleeping baby. "She looks as if she would be worth five cows."

"Ay, she will be worth more," answered Makanya proudly. "And Nomusa here, who helps me so well, is worth seven cows already."

Zitu looked at Nomusa appraisingly; then, taking hold of her firm arm, he said, "She is a strong girl, almost as big as her older brother. I hear she can do anything a boy can. If she were a boy, I would take her on the elephant hunt when we leave at the full moon."

At the full moon! thought Nomusa, her heart beating excitedly.

Inwardly she began counting the number of days to the full moon. About ten sleeps away, she said to herself. There will be time for one more visit from my father. How can I make him decide to take me? What can I do that will prove to him that I am more courageous than other girls, that I am strong and have no fear?

Half dreaming, she began to leave the hut.

"Where are you going, Nomusa?" asked her mother.

"To play *Hlungulu* with Themba," she murmured. "I promised him."

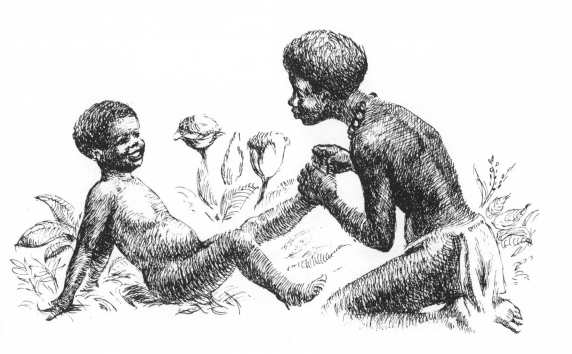

FOUR: Nomusa and Her Brothers

Hardly had Nomusa's head appeared at the entrance of the hut when Themba pounced on it, trying to get astride her neck, shouting, "My calf wins the race!"

"Get off, Themba!" Nomusa protested, though she had to laugh at him. "I'm no calf. And who told you about calf races? They are absolutely forbidden."

"Kangata told me. He said they have fun with calves in the pasture."

"How well I know it!" said Nomusa. "I wish I could spend my days in the pasture and have as good a time as my brothers do!"

"When I am big, I shall go to the pasture," said Themba proudly.

"Yes," Nomusa replied. "You are very lucky to be a boy. Girls' work is no fun at all."

"Play *Hlungulu*," begged Themba. "You promised."

"Very well, sit down over there," said Nomusa. "Now put your feet towards me.

> *"Hlungulu, hlungulu goduka*
> *Amas omntawana wakho adlive*
> *Adlive yig wababa*
> *Gwababa, gwababa goduka*
>   *Ubuye ngezotwasa."*

> *"Crow, Crow, go home.*
>   *Jackdaw has eaten*
> *Your babe's clotted milk.*
>   *Jackdaw, Jackdaw, go home.*
> *You will come back at the*
>   *new moon."*

Themba giggled as Nomusa acted out the song with grimaces and dramatic gestures. Before she had actually finished he was already begging, "Again, again!" When she had sung *Hlungulu* for the third time, he placed his wide, bare feet on Nomusa's lap and said, "Now sing me *ta-yi-ya-ne-lo.*"

Putting her thumb and forefinger on the big toe of his left foot, she began softly:

giving each toe a gentle squeeze. From the beginning of the song to the end, Themba's face was one delighted grin. As soon as she squeezed the last toe, he laughed and said, "More, Nomusa, more!"

At last it was time to stop. Nomusa had to grind
the corn for the mealie mush they would eat later.
Usually it was her mother who ground the corn, because it took strong arms; but since Nomusa knew her
mother was busy entertaining her father, she decided
to do it for her.

She picked up a small round stone lying next to a
larger one which was scooped out in the middle. Into
the scooped-out stone she threw a handful of hard
kernels of corn. Then, using the small round stone like
a rolling-pin and flicking a little water into the hollow
stone, she ground and ground the corn until it became
a coarse corn meal. When it was ground she poured it
into a basket where it would be ready when her mother
needed it for porridge or corn cakes. Part of it would
be brewed for her father's beer, as well.

Nomusa went on pounding and rolling the corn.
She grew tired and wiped off the moisture on her face
with the back of her hand. She wondered how her
mother managed to pound and pound for such long
periods without stopping. As she rested a moment, she
heard someone call, "Yo, Nomusa!"

She looked up and saw Sisiwe entering the kraal with a basket on her head. The green tops of vegetables showed above the top of the basket.

"Tired after the elephant hunt?" teased Sisiwe.

"I see you have been weeding your mother's garden," Nomusa remarked, ignoring the teasing.

"Yes," said Sisiwe. "And now I have to fetch water again. I'll never get ready in time for Damasi's party. I haven't even ground my paint yet. Have you?"

"No. I'll go with you to fetch water. Perhaps we'll find the right paint stones on the way."

Nomusa went back to finish grinding the corn while Sisiwe carried the basket of beans and sweet potatoes to her hut.

Soon Sisiwe came out again, looking more cheerful. This time she was carrying an empty water jar and eating something. Nomusa picked up a jar lying next to the thatch of her hut and walked over to meet her half sister, who offered her a piece of melon. Side by side, one with the water jar on her left hip, the other with it on her right, the girls proceeded to the stream.

"Our father has come," Nomusa said. "Ay, Sisiwe

he is as you said. We saw the new belt of wildcat tails,"

"And did he speak of the elephant hunt?" asked Sisiwe.

"Yes," replied Nomusa unhappily. "He said that if I were a boy he might have taken me along. If only I were! He will certainly take my brother, Mdingi. Well, at least I shall have the fun of taking the cattle to pasture while he is away, for Kangata is too young to watch them all by himself."

Nomusa began to grow excited at the prospect of taking the cattle to pasture and for a moment even thought it would make up for not being allowed to go on the elephant hunt.

"Oh, Nomusa, why must you always be so eager to do what boys do? You should be content with being a girl. Girls are worth much more than boys. No Zulu girl can be had for a wife unless she is paid for in cattle. We are valuable."

But Nomusa's mind was no longer on what Sisiwe was saying. Her eyes were searching the ground to right and left, seeking the stones with which to make the paint. Halfway to the stream, Nomusa and Sisiwe placed their empty jars under a mimosa tree and left the path to look for colored stones that were soft enough to grind.

"Here's a white one," called Nomusa to her sister. "And here's another. If we find two more white ones, we'll have enough for white paint."

When they had gathered all the stones they would need, Sisiwe said: "We'll leave them here in a pile until we come back from the stream."

"The water is much lower than it was this morning," Nomusa remarked. "How thirsty the sun must be to drink so much every day. Well, anyway, there's still enough for a good dip; and here I go!" In she dived, the pink soles of her feet gleaming. Sisiwe laughed and plunged in after her.

The two girls began to splash and pull each other under the water with so much shouting and merriment that birds nearby grew frightened and flew away. The monkeys hiding in the boughs lifted their heads and stared in wonder as the girls played in the water.

After a while, Nomusa and Sisiwe filled their jars with water and covered them with leaves from the bushes. They placed a cushion of rushes on top of their heads before balancing the jars on their heads. Then they rose carefully, first one knee, then the other, without spilling a single drop.

When they reached the spot where they had left their paint stones, the girls picked them up one by one

with their nimble toes, passing them to their hands.

When they got to their kraal, Nomusa and Sisiwe left the water in their huts. Then they sat in an open space near the huts, with their piles of stones before them. With a hard stone they pounded the soft red, black, and white stones, putting the different colors in separate piles, on leaves. Umpondo, Sisiwe's little brother, only a few days older than Themba, sat between his sisters, picking up the little pieces of soft stone as they pounded away. Nomusa said to him, "You may have some of the stones if you wish, little brother," and she pushed some of them toward him.

The soft paint stones crumbled to bits easily as Nomusa crushed and pounded them. After the pieces were small enough, she ground them until they were fine as dust. Nomusa and Sisiwe worked silently for a time. Then Umpondo said, "Nomusa, Themba said you know good stories. Do you know about Uthlakanyana?"

"Oh, yes," said Nomusa. "Mdingi has told me many stories about that dwarf and his magic. I don't know which one to tell you."

"Any one," begged Umpondo.

Without stopping what she was doing, Nomusa began, "*Za puma zenke izilwane, za li dhla; la ngobuhlunga bezinyoka, nezinyosi, naofezela neninyovu. La kala, lakala ke, la ze la fa* . . . Once upon a time Uthlakanyana took a bag to the forest. Inside of it he had a giant cannibal whom he had fought and defeated. As he walked along he found a snake, then a wasp, then a scorpion. All these biting and poisonous things he put into the bag with the giant. The giant said, 'Let me out, let me out. They are biting me.' They bit and bit him until he died. So he died."

"Do you know any others?" asked Umpondo eagerly.

"Yes, but not now."

Nomusa had now finished grinding her stones. She looked at her three little mounds of red, black, and white powder. "That's done," she said to Sisiwe. "We shall have enough to paint our whole bodies." Then she called out, "Look! Our brothers are already re-turning from the pasture. *Hau!* Mdingi, Kangata!"

Her own brothers were the last of the boys leading their mothers' cows and calves into the cattlefold inside the kraal. This was fenced off from the circle of huts by a thick wall of boughs and twigs. All the drainage from the huts flowed down to the cattlefold which was on the lower side of the sloping hill where the kraal was situated . In this cattlefold were also the mealie and grain pits where the corn was stored by the various wives after it had been stripped from the cobs. Nomusa's mother had told her that the fluids from the cattle percolated into the ground and turned the corn and grain sour. This prevented the weevils from eating it up.

As Nomusa proudly watched her mother's cows walking single file into the cattlefold, she noticed that her mother's favorite, Nyawuza, was not among them.

Where could she be?

Nomusa ran toward the cattlefold just as her brothers were entering it.

Mdingi saw her and called, "Go back, Nomusa! You know it's bad luck for girls to be here when we milk the cows."

"Yes, I know," Nomusa answered, looking at the cows to make sure she was not mistaken. "But did you bring back all of our mother's cows? I do not see Nyawuza."

Kangata stood next to Mdingi, looking solemn. Silently he gazed at his elder brother and sister. Mdingi's face was a study of misery and fear.

Nomusa knew something serious had happened.

FIVE: # A Lost Cow

At first Mdingi stood silent. Then he confessed.

"While we were resting after playing games, I began to think about a song. Sometimes when I do that I forget about everything else. It was like that today. When I looked for the cows, they had wandered off. I ran to drive them back, but I could not find Nyawuza. I left Kangata with the others while I searched for her. I looked and whistled until we had to come home. But I could not find the cow."

"It is my fault, too," Kangata said, stoutly. "I fell asleep. Oh, this is the worst thing that could happen! When Tahle lost a calf once he was punished severely."

Nomusa felt very sorry for her brothers, especially for Mdingi. Kangata might be scolded, but the cows were Mdingi's responsibility. If Nyawuza were not found, he would certainly be punished for his carelessness.

It was especially bad because Nomusa knew that their father frowned on Mdingi more often than on any of his children. Zitu himself was very strong and brave, and a great warrior and hunter. He was often disappointed in Mdingi. It was no secret that Mdingi liked making up songs and telling stories more than anything else.

Nomusa's heart filled with pity as she saw Mdingi's misery. She began to think of what might be done.

"If we wait till morning, Nyawuza may be killed by some animal. That would be a disgrace for you always, Mdingi."

"It is true," Mdingi acknowledged dejectedly.

"She must be found," Nomusa declared. "I shall go right away to look for her."

"But, Nomusa, it is growing dark! You would not be safe. Some wild animal might attack you!"

"I must find Nyawuza," Nomusa said firmly.

"Then I shall go with you," said Mdingi.

"No, no! You must milk the cows. And say nothing about this. Our father is in our hut now; if he hears what has happened he will be very angry. My work is finished; I shall not be missed."

"I cannot let you go alone," Mdingi protested. "Nyawuza knows my whistle."

"Show me how you whistle," directed Nomusa.

Mdingi whistled, and Nomusa imitated him. After a few tries she could do it exactly like Mdingi. Here is one more thing Nomusa can do as well as I, Mdingi thought bitterly. She should have been the boy.

"Do not say anything about the lost cow," Nomusa cautioned. "Tomorrow is the day of Damasi's party, and we might not be allowed to go."

Out of the kraal flew Nomusa like a small wild thing, her neck pocket bouncing as she ran. Her brothers watched her go, now worried about Nomusa as well as the cow.

" I should not have let her go," muttered Mdingi to Kangata as they went to the cattlefold to do the milking.

Nomusa ran along the deeply marked path which the cattle had made on their way from the kraal to the pasture. She wasted no time, but still her keen eyes saw signs that told what her brothers did in the pasture all day.

There were the remains of a fire. They must have caught some birds and roasted them. And perhaps they had taken some yams from their mothers' vegetable gardens. What a good time they must have had, thought Nomusa.

She could see large worn-out banana leaves on a small clay slope. These the boys had used as sleds for coasting. What fun it was, and how easy to find another banana-leaf sled when the old one was worn out!

Under a tree lay a large ball of leaves, twigs, and moss. Nomusa knew what that had been used for. Her brothers, lined up on two sides, had hurled pointed sticks at the ball as it rolled swiftly downhill.

Small wonder that Zulu boys grew up to be such great hunters with their spears and bows and arrows. Even little Themba had a toy bow and arrow with which he played at hunting. But he used the chickens

and dogs around the kraal as targets, much to the an-
noyance of his father's wives.

Nomusa came upon some long sticks standing
against the trunk of a tree. She had often seen the boys
play this game in their kraal in the evening. Standing
opposite his opponent, each boy would try to strike
the other's body, holding the stick in the middle so
that a large piece extended on each side of him. The
boys used all their speed and agility to try to ward off
the blows from their opponents' sticks. A player had
to be skillful indeed or he would soon be covered
with bruises.

As Nomusa had expected, the cow was nowhere
to be seen about the pasture. She began whistling loudly
and calling the cow with all her might.

"Nyawuza! Nyawuza!"

From a long way off came faintly the echo: "Nyawuza! Nyawuza!"

Nomusa decided she must go into the woods.
Where else could the cow have gone? Picking up a
pointed stick, Nomusa walked into the shadowy woods.

She whistled Mdingi's call over and over again.

HUGH STEPHENS LIBRARY
STEPHENS COLLEGE
COLUMBIA, MISSOURI

Moving between the well-spaced trees, she pushed aside with her stick the vines and creepers that came in her way. Once the whir of flying wings over her head gave her a great fright.

Only a bat! she thought, ashamed of her fear.

But the farther she went into the woods the less courageous she felt. She wished now that she had let Mdingi come with her. Oh, where could Nyawuza have gone? Was she perhaps already eaten by a lion or a hyena?

By this time Nomusa was deep in the woods. Her eyes had become so accustomed to the darkness that she was able to see where she was going quite well. She called and whistled, she slapped at trees with her stick to frighten off lurking animals. She had often heard that the rhinoceros hated loud noises and ran away at sudden sounds. She hoped it would frighten away other animals, too.

Once she saw some small glowing eyes peering at her from a bush. It made Nomusa's flesh creep with dread. The fast beating of her heart made her whistle tremble and quaver. Her throat suddenly went dry, and

112959

she found herself scarcely able to utter any sound whatever.

All at once, Nomusa heard a low and doleful moo from somewhere to the right of her. She plunged excitedly through the thicket in the direction of the sound. Another low, mournful moo.

Nomusa came to a small swamp; and there was Nyawuza. One foot was caught in a liana, and she was still struggling to free herself from the vine.

With a cry of joy and relief, Nomusa rushed up to the cow. She put her arms around her neck. "Nyawuza, our dear one, are you hurt?"

She bent down to examine Nyawuza's leg and to see how she could free her. Nyawuza had got herself more and more entangled with the vine by trying to free herself. First Nomusa pulled at it with all her strength, but soon she saw that it required cutting. She had no knife, so she tried using her pointed stick to get between the vines and the cow's leg. This hurt Nyawuza, and she frantically pulled herself away.

"What shall I do?" wondered Nomusa. She groped about on the ground looking for a rock with a sharp edge, feeling rather than seeing the stones. All at once she felt a sharp pain in her hand.

"A snake!" gasped Nomusa.

But it was not a snake bite after all, but a cut made by something sharp, perhaps the very thing she could use to cut the vine. Nomusa bent down, feeling about cautiously for the sharp object that had cut her.

Ah! She had it—a stone with a knifelike edge, half embedded in the earth. Nomusa dug it out, with some difficulty, and ran to Nyawuza. She knelt in front of the cow and held her leg firmly with one hand while she chopped at the vine with the stone.

Nyawuza looked on with melancholy eyes. The task of cutting the liana was not easy, though the stone was sharp. The vine was tough and full of sap, and it did not break easily. But Nomusa worked and worked at one place until she had cut it through. Finally Nyawuza was free.

By this time Nomusa was so tired that she felt as if the kraal were a hundred miles away. "Come, good Nyawuza. We must hurry home. Our mother is waiting."

On their dark journey homeward, Nomusa kept

up a conversation with the cow to reassure her. Now and then Nomusa stumbled over rough ground and unexpected bumps. Sometimes she was not at all sure which was the right direction, and she grew frightened at the thought of being lost.

It seemed a very long time before Nomusa felt under her feet the familiar path leading to her kraal.

Delighted to be so near home, she gave Nyawuza an affectionate and resounding slap on her rump.

The cow gave a sudden leap forward, and went galloping into the kraal, almost dashing against a group of Nomusa's older brothers and sisters.

But Nomusa did not stop to speak to them, for she must find Mdingi at once. It was long past the cow's milking time, and her udder was swollen.

Before Nomusa reached the cattlefold, Mdingi came rushing to meet her. "You found her!" he cried in relief. "I have been worried about you!" There was much more that Mdingi wanted to say, but Nomusa knew what he felt.

"Go quickly," she said gently. "Nyawuza needs milking."

"I go," Mdingi said.

Nomusa turned back to the other children, who were playing a spitting game. At a given signal, they passed their hands before their mouths, spitting on the palm as it passed. Then each child was given a chance to guess where the spit had hit the hand.

Nomusa watched for a few moments, but she was

too tired to play. As she was about to enter her hut, she saw her father sitting outside the entrance gazing at the rising moon and smoking his oxhorn pipe. Without turning his head, he said quietly, "I am glad you found the cow, my daughter."

Astonished, Nomusa said to herself, "By what magic does my father always manage to know everything that is happening in the kraal?"

Before unrolling her mat, Nomusa took some half-cooked pumpkin and some stewed meat from the pot. Drowsily she began to eat. Puleng came to help her, and together they finished the pumpkin and meat.

With one arm around her dog's neck, Nomusa stretched out her tired legs and fell sound asleep.

SIX

Preparing for the Party

The first thing Nomusa thought when she awoke was, "Today is the day of the party at Damasi's kraal! My work must be done quickly so I shall be ready to go this afternoon."

Mdingi and Kangata were now awake. Their eyes shone with excitement, and Nomusa knew that they too were thinking about the party. Because of it, they would start off to the pasture earlier today.

They helped themselves from the cook pot. Nomusa pushed more dry twigs on the smoldering fire so her mother could start cooking more food when the pot was empty. She and her brothers made sure there was enough food left for their mother and Themba when they awoke.

Out of the hut crawled Nomusa, Mdingi, and Kangata, one after the other, eating the food they held in their hands. They looked up at the sky to see what kind of day it was. Off in the distance Nomusa saw some threatening-looking clouds.

"Oh, it's not a nice day," she said, disappointed.

"That is true," replied Mdingi; "but it may clear up before we leave this afternoon."

"I think it's going to rain," said Kangata pessimistically.

"Come along, Kangata," ordered his big brother.

Nomusa was just leaving through the kraal gate when she heard one of her sisters calling, "Nomusa, wait for me!" It was Hlamba, the daughter of her father's third wife. Nomusa's mother was his fourth wife. Hlamba, too, was carrying a water jar, which she balanced expertly on her grass- skirted hip.

Nomusa waited until Hlamba caught up with her. *"Sakubona!"* she greeted her. "I am glad to have your company, sister. I see you are already wearing your new beads. They are beautiful! And is that the grass skirt you are wearing to Damasi's party?"

"Oh, no," said Hlamba loftily. "I am saving the new one until we go. But I just couldn't wait to wear the beads."

Hlamba was taller and plumper than Nomusa. Her body was beginning to take on the form of a woman, and she felt her importance now that her age required her to wear a grass skirt just like her mother's.

"When I am twelve years old, I suppose I shall have to wear a grass skirt, too," said Nomusa without any enthusiasm.

"Of course," said Hlamba. "You will be a woman then."

"A woman—in two years!" thought Nomusa. Somehow she could not feel happy about it. She wanted so much to play for a long, long time. She walked beside Hlamba for a while, not saying a word, but thinking a great deal. Hlamba kept a steady flow of conversation most of the way, but Nomusa hardly heard her. She kept talking about the designs she would put on her body for the party.

"And what designs and colors shall you paint on your body?" Hlamba was asking. This question interested Nomusa. All the way back to the kraal the conversation continued about the preparations for the party.

"Do you know that our sister Sisiwe has tattooed herself?" asked Nomusa.

"So soon? Did she use a pointed stick, or did she put the glowing embers on the cow dung over the skin?" inquired Hlamba.

"I saw her use a pointed stick. I hope the marks will last at least until the day after the party," said Nomusa.

"Yes, after all that work and pain of making the tattoo," said Hlamba sympathetically.

When Nomusa and Hlamba brought their water jars to their huts, the bigger boys were already in the cattle pasture. Only the smaller children were playing about in the kraal space. They were making toy kraals, cattle, and dolls out of clay and baking them in the sun.

There was Themba among the little boys, making clay oxen and cattle kraals and pretending to trade toy cattle for dolls as wives. That was what the men did.

While the small children played, the older girls were busy helping their mothers, and there was great activity inside and outside the huts.

Nomusa had finally finished weeding her mother's garden and had carried back in her left hand a large pumpkin. In her right she held three long pieces of sugar cane. Out of her mouth stuck a small piece of sugar cane which she was chewing and sucking as she walked briskly to her hut. She had stuck five gray and white porcupine quills in her thick hair. Carefully she dropped the pumpkin and the sugar cane before the hut entrance and pushed them before her as she crawled in.

"Well, today you have returned very quickly, Nomusa," her mother said approvingly. "Have you weeded the garden well?"

"That I have, my mother," said Nomusa. "And see what I have brought you"—pointing proudly to the quills in her hair.

Her mother stopped brewing corn beer and came over to examine the porcupine quills. She took one out of Nomusa's hair and put it into her own, trying it out by gently scratching her head with it.

"Yo! Very sharp point," she observed. "How did you get the quills?"

"While I was weeding the garden, I saw the porcupine close to the ground trying to creep out from under our thorn fence. So I threw a large yam at it as hard as I could, and although the porcupine got away, the yam lay on the ground with these porcupine quills in it."

Her mother laughed aloud. "You are as good a shot as your brothers. You would be a good hunter."

"I would rather be a good hunter than be allowed to wear a grass skirt," confessed Nomusa.

"Perhaps you can do both; but you will learn that it is good to be a woman, too. How are the crops? Are any pineapples ripe yet?"

"No, my mother. They are still hard and green. I felt all of them. But the beans will be ready by tomorrow, I am sure. I go now to gather wood for your fire."

"Very well, Nomusa. Hurry with your chores so you can prepare yourself for the party."

Nomusa smiled at her mother, grateful to her for understanding what was in her mind.

When she had returned with the firewood and ground some corn, her mother said, "You have done enough. The sun is now high, and it is time for you to paint and grease yourself."

Nomusa did not have to be urged twice. She took out her little piles of ground stone, which were lying neatly on large leaves, carried them carefully outdoors, and laid them on the shady side of the hut while she got some water and lamb fat. Leaving each color on its separate leaf, Nomusa poured water, drop by drop, first on the red powder, then on the black, then on the white, mixing each with a different thin twig. Into each color she stirred a little fat until it was just the right thickness. As if she were a chemist, she examined each color with the tip of her finger to see that it was neither too thin nor too thick, neither too light nor too dark. From time to time she tried a little of the color on her arm in order to see if it was just the right shade and would stay on well.

Finally Nomusa was satisfied. With some soft dried rabbits' paws that she used as paintbrushes, she began smearing her body, first putting on the red coat that made her skin a lovely warm copper color. She waited a few minutes for it to dry well. On top of the red paint she began putting the designs she had decided on long ago. The white circles were painted on first, then black circles put around these. Radiating from these she drew shapes of diamonds, squares, a series of wavy lines, and then dots. It was such a balanced pattern of design and color that an artist could not have done better. For her back she needed some help; so she called Sisiwe, who was coming out of her hut.

"What, you are all ready?" asked Sisiwe. "Why, I haven't even finished my work yet. I still have to get wood and grind some corn. It's a good thing the tattooing is done."

"I will help you with the corn, Sisiwe, if you paint my back the way I tell you to."

"I shall do it gladly, Nomusa."

Carefully, Nomusa stooped before Sisiwe's grinding stone, afraid lest she make cracks in the paint on her body. She began grinding the corn, throwing into the scooped stone a handful of dried kernels now and then. Sisiwe, more cheerful now, ran quickly out of the kraal for the wood.

While Nomusa worked, she could not help admiring herself, and her eyes wandered up and down the front of her body. Nomusa was pleased with her designs. When she had given her body a final layer of grease to protect and bring out the colors of the paint and had put on all her bangles and bracelets, she would look beautiful indeed. She would not forget to wear her new oxhide neck-pocket, either. Already she had put into it most of her best treasures, to be exchanged for even better ones, she hoped, with Damasi's guests.

It did not seem at all long before Sisiwe was back again, her arms filled with branches and twigs. She dropped her load behind her hut, then carried into the hut as much wood as her mother would need for several hours. Out she ran to Nomusa and squatted beside her, taking the grinding stone out of her hand.

"I can go on grinding if you will get my paints and cover my back with red paint," said Nomusa.

Sisiwe darted over to Nomusa's hut to gather up the paints. When she returned, Nomusa said, "I think the paints will need more water. They are a little dry now. When you have used what you need on my back, you may have the rest of the colors for yourself."

"You are good, Nomusa." Sisiwe added some water to the paint, stirring water and paint together with great care. She began covering Nomusa's back with the red color as smoothly as she could. Nomusa giggled as the rabbit's foot tickled her sides.

After having made the designs and used the colors

Nomusa showed her, Sisiwe said, "It is done now, and you look splendid."

"I can help you with your back, just as you did mine," said Nomusa. With Nomusa's help it did not take long for Sisiwe to be completely painted. Nomusa then went back to her hut to get her bangles and beads. She reappeared before Sisiwe wearing them around her waist, her neck, her elbows, her upper arms, her ankles, the calves of her legs, and her knees. She was now well greased, too, and glistened in the sun. Her bulging ox-hide neck-pocket, soft and new, hung around her neck. A thin circlet of white, green, and red beads surrounded her pretty head.

As her little brothers and sisters saw Nomusa approach they stopped everything they were doing. Excitedly they crowded around to examine her decorations and adornments and point out to one another the extraordinary designs on her body. They touched her shiny bangles, her beads and bracelets, all of which she had made herself.

"How I wish I could go to Damasi's party, too," said one of her small admirers. "Did you make this bracelet?" asked another. "Where did you get those beads?"

Puleng returned from some little adventure he had been having and began to bark at Nomusa, disturbed over her strange appearance. What with his barking and the shouting and loud questions of all the children crowding round Nomusa and Sisiwe, there was such a din that mothers stuck their heads out of the entrance of their huts and crossly commanded, *"Tula!"*

"Hush!" warned Nomusa. "You will wake all the babies." She stroked Puleng's head to reassure him and quiet his barking.

"Here come the others, ready for the party," announced Sisiwe. "Oh, look!"

Nineteen boys and girls—painted, greased, bedecked with all kinds of beads and bangles encircling almost every part of the body—began gathering at the kraal entrance ready to set forth. Some of the girls wore grass skirts; some of the boys were wearing antelope belts for the first time and were proudly fingering and arranging them. Some had feathers stuck in their hair. Faces were painted with designs meant to terrify and amuse.

Nomusa and Sisiwe joined their older sisters and brothers at the kraal entrance. They were ready to start for the party now. The smaller children, who were being left behind, began jumping and shouting around them, cheering as they left.

The morning haze had disappeared, and Damasi's kraal could now be seen clearly on the hill beyond. As Nomusa walked along with her nineteen excited brothers and sisters, she fingered her neck-pocket and began to think of Damasi and how glad she would be to see him.

Damasi's Party

The distance to Damasi's kraal was quite far, but it did not seem so to Nomusa or to her brothers and sisters as they walked toward it, single file. Far off, they saw a thin line of children coming in their direction. They, too, were on their way to the party. Nomusa wondered how many children would be at Damasi's party. Maybe a hundred.

Kangata was terribly excited about going to a party in a neighboring kraal. It was his first one.

"We are near now, Nomusa, are we not?" he asked.

"Yes," she answered. She began to laugh as she looked at her small brother's face, for it was marked and painted in such a curious and grotesque manner that his nose looked as if it had been divided in two.

Kangata looked offended and put his grubby hand up to his face to discover the cause of Nomusa's mirth. Nomusa quickly reassured him. "You have certainly made a design like that of no other. Perhaps you will win a prize."

When the children neared the thorn fence surrounding Damasi's kraal, Zabala walked forward quickly to lead the line of twenty brothers and sisters, all children of Nomusa's father. Zabala, whose mother was called Great Wife because she was Zitu's first wife, would be chief of Nomusa's kraal some day, because he was Zitu's eldest son.

Standing just within the entrance of the kraal to greet the guests as they entered were Damasi's father and uncle and their wives. They pointed out the huts that had been reserved for the party.

Nomusa found Kangata close at her side, his eyes wide with curiosity, trying to see everything in the strange kraal at once. Delicious smells of food cooking filled the air and made Kangata's mouth water.

Nomusa began straightening the halo of beads around her head, adjusting some of the bangles that had got twisted on the way. Most of her sisters were arranging their short grass skirts and bead kilts, too.

Zabala walked up to the entrance of Damasi's hut, followed by his nineteen brothers and sisters. He stood tall before the hut, legs apart, arms by his side, and loudly cleared his throat. "A-hem!" But there was so much noise in the hut, and such excitement, that no one, it seemed, had heard his announcement of their arrival. Again he cleared his throat, this time more loudly, with a reinforcement of "A-hems" from behind him. Zabala glowered at those who had given him this unwanted help.

This time they were heard. There was a sudden hush within. Almost immediately a fantastic-looking head, stuck full of small birds' feathers, green, blue, yellow, and red, appeared in the entrance. It was Damasi. *"Sakubona! Sakubona!"* he said, smiling.

"Usaphila! Usaphila!" called the guests from Nomusa's kraal.

Chief for the day, Damasi was in charge of everything. He quickly beckoned to everyone to enter. First went Zabala. Then, one by one, all the brothers and sisters crawled in after him on hands and knees.

At first the children from Nomusa's kraal were shy, but soon they began to mingle freely with the other guests. Waves of noise surged up in the hut. More guests arrived, making the hut hotter and noisier than ever. The boys wandered over to one side of the hut, and the girls stayed at the other.

Nomusa went to look at a calf that was tied in a corner of the hut. It was only a few days old and still too young to be taken to pasture. Together with a young goat, it was being kept as a pet. Girls did not often have a chance to be with cows and calves, and Nomusa enjoyed petting the calf.

Several dogs which had followed some of the children to the party ran in and out, between and over the legs of the smaller guests, looking for pieces of food that had been dropped on the floor. Every little while there was a fight between two dogs when both snatched at the same morsel.

Their barking, snapping, and growling frightened

the chickens that had wandered in. Flapping their wings in terror, they crowed and cackled, one or two flying onto the backs of the shrieking children.

This caused more excitement, laughter, and

screeching, until the poor little calf began to strain at its grass rope in an effort to get away. Nomusa patted her. "Do not be afraid, little calf. I will not let anyone hurt you."

While she was talking to the calf, Damasi's sister Intombi, a year older than Nomusa, came up to her and said, "It is a fine calf. Do you like it?"

"Who would not?" answered Nomusa. "She will be a beautiful cow." Then, seeing Intombi's bulging neck-pocket, she pointed to it. "What have you in there?"

"I will gladly show you," said Intombi. "But you must show me what is in your pocket, too."

Nomusa opened her neck-pocket and drew from it a red and green feather, now somewhat bent—the one she had found at the stream.

"M-m-m-m!" said Intombi, admiringly. "What else have you?"

Nomusa's fingers probed the depths of her pocket. She brought out a lovely bead of clay, brown, with a red and yellow border. The bead was no bigger than a small grape. "I made it myself," explained Nomusa.

"I found a very special kind of clay, mixed the colors, and then baked it in the sun. Do you like it?"

"I do," said Intombi. "If you will part with it, I will give you this." She quickly loosened her bulging neck-pocket and took out something brown, spotted with white. It looked very soft and furry.

"Why, it's a deer mouse!" cried Nomusa. "Where did you get it?"

"I found it nibbling in my mother's garden. If you like it, you may have it in exchange for the bead."

"Be careful not to drop the bead, for it may break." Nomusa said, handing it to Intombi and taking the deer mouse.

"It's not alive, you know," Intombi said, as she saw Nomusa carefully examining her new treasure.

"Is it still good to eat?" Nomusa asked.

"That I do not know, but the fur can be used."

Intombi opened her neck-pocket wide and showed Nomusa all the bits of stone, feathers, bangles, and other trinkets that she carried around with her. Suddenly Intombi sprang up. "Oh, they are starting another game. Let us play, too, Nomusa."

"What are they playing?"

"Husbands and wives. It's lots of fun. I hope Zabala chooses me." Intombi moved closer to the line of boys so that Zabala would not fail to see her. She looked smilingly at him until he caught her eye.

How tiresome to play such a game, thought Nomusa. I should much prefer going outside.

She was standing apart, watching the good-natured scramble of the boys picking their girls, not once thinking about a partner for herself. Suddenly she felt someone tapping her shoulder insistently. "You are my wife for this game," Damasi said. "Now let me see if you are a good one."

"And let me see if you are a good husband," replied Nomusa.

The girls picked up little grass mats and baskets and filled them with food for themselves and their "husbands."

Damasi said to Nomusa, "I hear you can do all the things that a boy can do. Are you a good cook, too? That is more important."

"You shall see," answered Nomusa. "But you

must promise to go outside with me afterwards to shoot at targets." She set to work to prepare a dish that would not take very long. Soon she gave Damasi a mixture of chicken, corn, pumpkin, goat meat, and fried locust.

"Very good," said Damasi. "Now pass me the *amasi.*" These were the delicious curds of clotted milk that Nomusa liked so much. They were excellent for cooling and for quenching one's thirst. When Damasi had finished, he belched and said, "Soon we'll see if you are as good a hunter as you are a cook."

"Let us go outside now," Nomusa suggested, "if you have finished eating."

Together they left the hut. Damasi went into one of the other huts and brought out two bows and some arrows. One bow he handed to Nomusa.

"See if you can hit that branch," he said, pointing.

Nomusa stood straight and drew her right arm back with a quick pull. Off sped the arrow, straight into the middle of the thick branch.

"Good!" shouted Damasi. "We'll each take five turns and see how many hits we make."

As Damasi took a shot, Nomusa saw a bird flying

about a hundred yards away. Quickly she let the arrow go, and down went the bird.

"Not many boys your age can shoot a bird on the wing," said Damasi admiringly. "Where did you practice shooting?"

"In my mother's garden," answered Nomusa.

Just then Mdingi appeared. "Let me shoot," he said.

"Let us take turns shooting," said Nomusa. "You first, Damasi. Then Mdingi, then I."

Damasi let his arrows fly swiftly, one after the other. "Three out of five," announced Nomusa, running to pick up the fallen arrows.

"Your turn, Mdingi," said Damasi.

Taking careful aim, Mdingi shot his five arrows. "Four out of five!" he shouted.

Nomusa aimed and shot. "Three out of five, like me, Nomusa," Damasi said.

By now the younger children had grown tired of being husbands and wives—especially the girls, since they had to do all the work for the boys. The smaller girls began to play with clay dolls, and the little boys ran outdoors to play horse.

Sisiwe came up to Nomusa. "What will everyone think of you, playing with boys, shooting at a mark," she scolded. "You make us ridiculous with your tomboy ways! What good will it do you to know how to trap and shoot? You will never be allowed to go on a hunt. It is better for you to know how to be a good wife."

Nomusa left Damasi and went to sit with the girls from neighboring kraals. Bored, she listened to stories about things that had been going on in their kraals since the last time they had seen each other: about new babies, accidents to brothers or sisters, what vegetables were growing in their mothers' gardens, and such things. Body designs were compared and discussed, grass skirts felt, beads admired, and new teeth examined.

There was no special hour for eating. Children wandered in and out of the hut to get what they wanted. It was a never-ending feast.

Runaway Prize

Nomusa went into the warm hut for some pumpkin, but she came out quickly. She drew in a long breath of fresh air and wiped her perspiring brow.

"Oh, how good the night air feels!" she said to Intombi. "The moon is high, and the stars are sparkling already."

The cry of a very young baby was heard. Nomusa looked at Intombi.

"My uncle's wife has a new baby, born eight days ago. Should you like to see her?"

Nomusa was glad to accept the invitation. She loved babies, and she was glad to get away from the gossiping girls.

Together they walked over to the hut. In front of the entrance, Intombi turned to Nomusa. "Here are the ashes of the magic herb in which you must rub your feet before entering. You have come a long way, and you may have got something evil on them. With new babies we have to be very careful, you know."

Nomusa obediently rubbed her feet in the ashes while Intombi gave a polite cough, which was answered from within by a quiet, friendly *"Bayete."*

Nomusa and Intombi entered the hut. Nomusa smiled as she caught sight of the new baby, who was still moist from her bath.

"It is Nomusa," said Intombi simply to the baby's mother.

Nomusa's delight in the baby was plain to see; in a few moments she took off one of her necklaces of small shells and hung it around the baby's plump neck.

"It is a present for the baby," Nomusa said to the mother. "She is strong and big for her age. I hope she will grow up to be clever in boys' work as well as in girls'."

"We had not chosen a name for her," said the

mother, surprised at Nomusa's wish, "but now I know what it will be. We shall call her Nomusa, which means kindness, for you."

At these words Nomusa blushed so that her face had an even more beautiful color. It was the first time such an honor had been done her, and she was pleased and proud.

Soon after, Nomusa and Intombi left to join the other children. They found them all assembled in a huge circle in the kraal space. Damasi was in the center going from one child to another examining body designs.

"Hurry, get into the circle, or it will be too late," shouted Kangata impatiently when he saw Nomusa coming along.

She and Intombi lost no time in squeezing in next to some of the bigger girls, adding their laughter and chatter to that of the others as they waited for Damasi to finish judging the designs.

"Among the boys," announced Damasi finally, "the prize goes to Fanase. Among the girls"—and he hesitated for the moment as if making up his mind— "the prize goes to Nomusa."

Unbelieving, Nomusa looked at Intombi and then turned her head in the direction of Kangata. His face was full of disappointment and misery. Sad for her little brother, Nomusa could take no pleasure in having been awarded a prize. Just as she was thinking, "I shall give Kangata my prize," she heard Damasi shouting out loudly, "The prize for the funniest design goes to Kangata!"

There was a roar of laughter. The children clicked their tongues, *"tsick tsick,"* in congratulation. For a few moments Kangata did not know whether to laugh or to cry, but when Damasi called him into the large ring of children and handed him a basket full of roasted winged ants, locusts, and caterpillars, his face broke into a cheerful grin, and he began to laugh, too. This caused the other children to laugh still more, and soon the kraal echoed with their pleasure. Nomusa expected to hear some of the mothers shout *"Tula!"* from their huts, but no one did. It was Damasi's party, and the children could do as they pleased for this one day.

"Come into the ring, Nomusa," called Damasi, "so everyone can see your designs." More emphatic "*tsick tsicks*" clicked around her. A little embarassed, she took Kangata's hand and then looked down toward her wriggling toes.

"I wonder what you're going to get," whispered Kangata. But Nomusa neither answered nor looked up. Her only desire was to be allowed to get out of the middle of the ring and go back to Intombi's side at once. What took Damasi so long? This was a poor joke—leaving her there next to Kangata with all those children staring at her. Kangata, however, was unconcerned. He was eating a locust with great relish and trying at the same time to count the number of delicacies he had won.

All at once the children grew silent. Nomusa looked up to see Damasi coming toward her with a very small gray striped monkey clinging to his neck with both little hands. When she saw the monkey, Nomusa's heart began to beat faster.

"For you," she heard Damasi saying, as he gently unclasped the monkey's arms from around his neck and handed him to Nomusa.

She murmured her thanks and tenderly took the

little animal in her arms. She could hardly believe she had won such a marvelous prize.

The girls crowded around Nomusa, trying to pet the little monkey. But he clung to Nomusa.

"See, he loves you already," said Intombi. "What are you going to call him?"

"He is striped like a zebra," Nomusa said, still in a sort of daze. "I think I shall call him Dube."

"I am happy because you like your prize," said Damasi in a low voice.

"Oh, thank you, Damasi! Indeed I like him very much! It is the best present I have ever had."

The sun had set long ago. Whatever the mellow light of the moon did not reach was bathed in darkness. As Nomusa stood holding Dube and petting him, Sisiwe came to her.

"Look, Nomusa. They are bringing out the drums. That means we shall soon begin to dance."

"Oh, I had better go right away and tie Dube in one of the huts so he won't run away."

Nomusa carried Dube into one of the empty party huts. He did not like it when Nomusa put him in a corner and tied a cord around his neck. The sound of drums from outside frightened Dube. He clung to Nomusa's leg as if begging her not to leave him. The drums sounded again.

"Oh, the dance!" cried Nomusa. Torn between her desire to stay with Dube and her eagerness to go to the dance, she pleaded. "Oh, Dube, I really can't stay any longer!"

Dropping the monkey on the floor, she rushed out to join the dancers. She fell in with one of the rows of children who were already hopping along rhythmically on one leg and chanting *"khelekhelekobe ngajlatshwa ameva"* to the beat of a pot drum.

It was nothing but a large earthenware pot with a goatskin drawn tightly over the mouth of it. Damasi's cousin, Bongoza, was playing it by tapping it with the palm and fingers of his hand. The excited and varied rhythms he produced threw the dancers into a joyful frenzy; they hopped first on one leg, then on the other, shouting and chanting.

After this dance had stopped, Damasi appeared with a bow made of a bent reed which he had strung tight with an ox-tendon string. He held one end of the bow in his lips and twanged the string with his thumb. This was the signal for another dance, and the children sprang up again.

The dancers got in a long line, and this time they composed their own dance. They turned to each other, grunting and screwing up their faces. Such hideous grimaces as they made! It was terrifying enough to scare away a lion, Nomusa thought. Soon she decided it was more fun to drop out of the dance and watch it. She singled out Kangata, whose movements and dreadful faces were so comical that Nomusa's sides ached from laughing.

"Oh, that Kangata!" she exclaimed. "What awful faces!"

Intombi had dropped out, too. "Let us get some corn kernels so we can play the game of guessing bird names," she suggested.

Nomusa went with her to a pile of dried mealie cobs. They began stripping off kernels and dropping them into a basket. When they had enough, the girls carried the basket out to an open space. Together they laid the kernels in rows on the ground.

From all sides came the children, eager to take part in the new game. *"Bula Msense!"* they called to each other, announcing the game.

"Boys on one side, girls on the other," cried Intombi.

The smaller children did not take part in this game; so they stood to one side watching the others. Each child was given a turn at naming a bird for each kernel, picking up a kernel if he could offer a name no other child had yet given. If he could not name a different bird, he had to drop out of the game.

At the beginning the corn kernels disappeared quickly as a child from one side would call out "finch," and the other side would cry "honey-bird," or "white-eye," or "woodpecker," or "nightjar."

Nomusa marveled at the number of birds the children knew. She was ashamed of having been eliminated when the game was not yet half over. Mdingi was still going strong against Damasi, Zabala, and Bongoza. Nomusa was very proud of him. Excitedly the onlookers cheered on the remaining contestants.

Presently it was announced that Mdingi was the winner. Intombi brought him a narrow belt of oxhide, with beads dangling from it; and everyone cheered as Mdingi delightedly fastened it around his slim waist.

It was now the turn of the smaller children to have a dance or game of their own. Kangata boldly walked into the empty space and began showing a new dance he had invented. As he chanted, he jumped up, at the same time kicking his buttocks with his bare heels. The other children imitated him.

It was a strenuous dance, and as the children grew tired, their throats became parched and they uttered their songs in short gasps. Weak corn beer and *amasi* were passed around to quench their thirst.

One of the older boys now came up, playing a flute made of the chinbone of a reedbuck. He sat on the ground and made up plaintive tunes while the children gathered around him, munching kaffir plums, blackberries, wild figs, or roasted caterpillars. The soothing music of the flute calmed the children and made the little ones so sleepy that they dozed off and had to be carried into the huts and laid on mats to sleep.

It was now midnight, and the moon floated behind some wispy clouds, making them luminous and gray. The older boys left the kraal and went off by themselves. Nomusa decided that instead of joining a girl's game she would go to the hut where she had left Dube.

Softly she groped her way among sleeping children to Dube's corner, expecting him to jump into her arms. But he did not come to her. He must be asleep, Nomusa thought. She was glad, for it made her feel less selfish for having left him.

It was quite dark in the corner, so she began feeling for Dube. At last she found the cord. But there was no monkey attached to it. With a sudden pang Nomusa realized that Dube might have run away.

Quietly, so as not to waken the sleeping children, she moved about the hut, hoping to find Dube hiding. But he was not there. Nomusa left the hut, wondering what to do. She decided to search in all the huts, and began by entering the main one, where the girls were busy playing *ngelitshe.*

"Yo, Nomusa!" they called. "Have you been in the hills with the boys, or have you been asleep in one of the huts with the little ones?"

Nomusa smiled wretchedly, and Intombi said, "Come and play with us, Nomusa. You will beat us all at this stone game. Here, take my stones for a while. I am tired." Nomusa wanted to say that she was weary of all these boring girls' games, but instead she squatted beside Intombi, taking the five stones.

Her heart was heavy as she held the stones in her hand. The game was to hold all the stones in one hand, tossing one into the air while holding all the others and catching the stone in the same hand. Each time a different stone was thrown. When a player failed to catch a stone, she was eliminated from the game. It was easy for Nomusa. She did not feel like playing, and as soon as the attention of the girls was turned from her, her eyes roamed over every part of the hut, searching for Dube. In an absent-minded way she tossed her stones, turning her head from side to side and then back, just in time to catch the tossed stone in her hand again.

After a while Nomusa decided to leave the hut. She gave the stones back to Intombi and crept out into the cool air of the starlit night. The girls continued with their game, forgetting about Nomusa.

Wild Boar

Outdoors it was dark and still. Who could find a monkey now? From somewhere far off Nomusa could hear the shouts of the older boys. In the waning moonlight she began walking toward the huts in which she had not made a search. How thankful she was that there were still places to search.

Walking toward the hut nearest the kraal entrance, she was suddenly startled by a long black shadow that seemed to withdraw hastily as she approached. Nomusa stood still, frightened but curious. Something was prowling outside the kraal fence. There was no doubt of that.

Again the shadow passed the kraal entrance, as if deciding whether it should come in or not. Nomusa felt goose flesh creep over her whole body. Was it a wild animal about to attack them? What should she do? She had no weapon with which to drive it off or kill it. She wanted to run or shout for help. The children might be in great danger if she did not act quickly. But if she screamed to attract the attention of Damasi's father and uncle, she might cause whatever it was to rush in at once and attack.

Again she saw the indistinct form. At the same
time, as the moon reappeared from under the clouds,
Nomusa's eye caught the glint of something long and
pointed lying next to one of the huts. Could it be a
spear? What a lucky thing if it was a weapon of some
kind! When the shadow disappeared again and the
moon floated under the clouds once more, Nomusa
dashed to the object she hoped was a spear. Yo! It was.
She picked it up just as if she had been accustomed to
holding such weapons all her life. Nomusa did not
doubt for a moment that she would know how to handle
it. Often enough she had watched the men and boys
throwing spears. Secretly she had even practiced with
long, heavy sticks.

She felt the point of the spear with her finger. It
was very sharp. She began moving cautiously. Nomusa's
hair fairly stood on end as she saw that the black thing
was a wild boar. Only too well she knew how fierce
a wild boar could be. Every Zulu feared and hated this
vicious beast with his dangerous tusks. Standing with
her back flattened against the kraal fence, close to the
entrance, with spear up and ready, Nomusa hid in the

deep shadow. She waited tensely for the boar to venture in. The wind, fortunately, was blowing in such a direction that the boar couldn't get her scent. Her upraised arm trembled a bit, then became steady as she waited.

Soon the boar's ugly head appeared within the kraal entrance not far from Nomusa. He had decided to come in. It was a rare chance for him. Ordinarily the kraal fence was entirely closed, but tonight, because the older boys were out, the kraal gate was left open for them. Slowly the beast moved his clumsy body through the kraal entrance. Once within, he lowered his head as if he had got a whiff of something and, with a snort, got ready to rush in the direction of the hut where the girls were playing *ngelitshe*.

There was no time to lose. With all her might, Nomusa hurled her spear at the neck of the boar. *Hau!* The spear caught him in the throat. With an enraged snort, he rushed toward Nomusa, the spear still sticking in his neck. He stumbled, and got up again. His roars, mingled with grunts of pain, woke up Damasi's father and uncle, as well as everyone else who had been asleep. Intombi and Sisiwe rushed out of the hut, followed by the other girls. When they saw the wounded boar they ran behind the hut.

The boar had now fallen, close to one of the huts. He made powerful efforts to raise himself and almost got up, when Damasi's father dashed up. He let fly an arrow from his bow, and the boar fell dead.

Nomusa ran to the side of Damasi's father. "How glad I am you came!"

Amazed, he asked, "Was it you who hurled the spear?"

Nomusa nodded.

Everyone crowded round the dead boar in astonishment.

Damasi's father said: "Nomusa is a brave girl. It was she who discovered the boar and wounded him. She has saved us from great danger. I shall tell her father, Chief Zitu, about her bravery."

There were loud cries of agreement. "Hau! Yo!"

Damasi's father put his arm around Nomusa's shoulder. "Come and rest. You are weary."

She followed him obediently. Unrolling a mat in the

little hut occupied by Damasi's mother and his baby brother, she threw herself upon it, exhausted. Only now did Nomusa realize fully the great danger she had been in and how lucky she had been. Oh, how tired and sleepy she was! Yawning, she put her arm under her head as a pillow and was about to fall asleep when there flashed through her mind the memory of her lost monkey, whom she had forgotten in all the excitement.

Her eyes filled with tears and she tried to swallow the lump in her throat. She buried her head in her arms. The joy of the day was entirely gone. Though she had been a brave hunter but a short time before, now she was only a small girl crying bitterly over a lost pet.

At last she dozed off and fell to dreaming of her search through deep and dangerous forests for her little monkey.

Muttering restlessly, Nomusa tossed from side to side in her sleep. She put her hand on her neck to scratch herself. Suddenly she felt something soft and warm moving across her shoulders and the back of her neck. She woke up with a start and clutched at the thing with both hands. There was a squeal of pain as she pulled it forward. Her fright turned to joy as she saw that what she held in her hand was the tail of a monkey. Dube!

"Oh, I have hurt you!" cried Nomusa, taking Dube in her arms and hugging him.

Damasi's mother smiled and said, "I am glad you like the little monkey. Damasi went to a great deal of trouble to get him when he was tending the cows in the pasture. He kept him as a pet for himself until you won him as a prize."

Just then Damasi's baby brother wailed. "*Tula!* We must be quiet now," warned Damasi's mother, and then, lying down on the mat next to the baby, she began nursing him. Soon he fell asleep again. Nomusa lay down on her mat, too, drawing Dube close to her.

"Where did you go to, you bad little Dube?" she whispered to him affectionately.

"Tchirk? Tchirk?" Dube answered, snuggling beside her. The warmth of his body next to her shoulder soothed Nomusa into a sleep from which she did not waken until she heard loud calls of "Come! Come! Time to go back to our kraals. Hurry, we are going!"

The sun was just rising above the horizon. The sky was lined with rose and deep blue, but the early morning air was cool, and the waiting children jumped about to keep warm. Pink and red flowers dotted the fields a short distance away, and a few birds were beginning to twitter.

The older boys straggled back into their groups exhausted and irritable because they had not slept all night. But they were aroused into curiosity by cries of "Did you hear? Don't you know?"

"What? What? Tell us," they demanded eagerly.

"Nomusa and her wild boar. She hit it with a spear. You can see it over there—behind the cattle kraal."

Those who had not yet seen the dead boar ran off at once, to return full of astonishment. They all agreed Nomusa was as good as any boy. Sisiwe had to admit that it was lucky for all of them that Nomusa liked shooting and hunting.

Nomusa was surrounded by the girls in her group, who gazed upon her with pride and envy. What a lot she would have to tell Themba! She could hardly wait to see his face when she showed him the monkey. She knew he would ask her to tell him the story of the boar over and over again.

There was a loud whistle. The children fell into lines, waving good-by to Damasi and his brothers and sisters and cousins. Tired and bedraggled, the children marched off. Some pushed each other ill-humoredly and quarreled on the way home, but finally they reached their kraals in time to begin their various duties—the boys going off to the pasture, the girls to their tasks. The boys hoped to make up their lack of sleep while tending the cows; but the girls knew they would have to wait until evening before they slept again. As soon as Nomusa entered her kraal with her brothers and sisters, she went directly to her hut to start her work.

In a few moments Nomusa was out of the hut again, headed for the stream with Dube perched on the empty water jar that rested on her hip. She fairly danced along the path as she looked at Dube and thought, "Never will my trips for water be tiresome again." She tweaked his ear gently, and Dube looked up at her and said, "Tchirk, tchirk."

TEN: # Zitu's Messenger

For most of the children, the days that
followed the party seemed like all other days. But not
for Nomusa. She had Dube.

Sometimes she took him with her when she went
to the stream. But often she left him behind with
Themba, who loved the little monkey almost as much
as Nomusa did.

One morning Nomusa was sitting with Themba
and Dube outside their hut, telling her little brother
the story of Damasi's party and the wild boar. Already
she had told it to him dozens of times, but Themba still
loved to hear it.

"Nomusa!" called Makanya.

Nomusa crawled inside the hut. Her mother was feeding Bala.

"When you weed the garden today, I want you to see what vegetables and fruits will be ready to pick in the morning," said Makanya. "Tomorow is the day for your father's visit. He may not be coming again for some time, and I want him to remember this visit."

"Is my father going on the elephant hunt soon?" Nomusa asked.

"Yes, but I do not know when. He will send a messenger to the headmen of the neighboring kraals."

"How I wish I could go with him!" Nomusa said.

"This is foolish, Nomusa," her mother said, almost sharply. "You know girls do not go on elephant hunts. If anyone from our hut went, it would be Mdingi."

"I know," answered Nomusa, softly.

"Why can't you be happy with girls' work like Sisiwe and the others? What your father hears about your skill and courage may please him, but it would be better if he heard it about your brother than about you. When it is time for you to marry, people will say, 'I wonder how many cows Nomusa will have to give for a husband,' rather than how many cows a husband will give for you."

Nomusa laughed. "I do not wish to marry at all. I wish always to stay with you."

The mother smiled as she fed Bala clotted milk. "Yes, yes, you think so now," she replied.

When Nomusa left the hut, Themba called eagerly, "Are you going to play with me, Nomusa?"

"No, I must weed our mother's garden."

"Well, tell me a story, then," pleaded Themba.

"When I come back. I shall take Dube with me, and you play with Umpondo."

When she returned, there was Themba waiting for her. "What about my story?" he demanded.

"Oh, I am so tired now!" said Nomusa.

"You can rest while you tell me the story," Themba suggested.

"All right. Wait till I get a drink for Dube and me."

When Nomusa came out, Themba quickly made room for her next to him. "Well, what's the story going to be about?" he asked, eyes bright with anticipation.

Nomusa thought for a moment, wondering what story to tell. "How would you like to hear about the hyena that tried to eat the moon?"

"Oh, I should like that," Themba assured her.

"Once upon a time," said Nomusa, "a hyena chanced upon a bone. She took it up in her jaws and carried it away.

"It happened that the moon was shining very brightly and the water in the stream was very still. The greedy hyena saw the moon's reflection in the quiet water. Thinking it was a fine big piece of meat, she threw aside her bone in order to grasp it.

"Into the water the hyena plunged her head. But she withdrew it with her mouth empty. The water was now disturbed, and the disappointed hyena could see nothing.

"She sat quietly on the bank, watching the stream. The water became clear again and reflected the image of the moon. The hyena made a fierce spring into the stream, trying to grasp the moon and hold it fast. But she seized only water and returned to the bank with her jaws empty, while the stream became muddy again.

"In the meantime, another hyena had picked up the bone from the bank and had quietly gone away with it. The first hyena kept on snapping at the water until morning came and the moon grew pale and could no longer be seen in the stream. Only then did the hyena look for the bone she had thrown aside to grasp for the moon. The bone was gone.

"Day after day the angry hyena returned to the stream, tramping the bank and muddying the water. Everyone laughed as they saw her run into the stream again and again, snapping and snapping her jaws and catching only water."

Nomusa looked at Themba, who was leaning drowsily against the hut. "Did you like the story?"

"Hm?" murmured Themba, rousing himself. "If that is the end of the story, I have heard you tell better ones. But thank you," he added, rising. "I see Somcuba. I am going to play *Ama-hu* with her."

The next morning when Nomusa and her mother were preparing the food they heard an odd commotion outdoors. They went out to see what it was about.

"Look at Kangata!" cried Themba.

Kangata was indeed a sight to see. His arms were covered with red circles, and he carried branches of wild cabbage in his arms.

"My father has chosen me to deliver an important message to all the kraals in our neighborhood," said Kangata, proudly holding aloft his branches of wild cabbage. "I am big now; so I am allowed to run and tell them that the elephant hunt is to be two sleeps away."

"You must tell them where the hunters are to meet and when," advised Nomusa. "As soon as they see the wild cabbage in your hand they will know your errand. Remember you must not speak until you are asked. Then tell when and where the hunters are to meet."

"And how does my boy-girl know all this?" asked Makanya, amused. "It is a pity your father did not choose you as messenger, since you know so well how hunting messages should be given."

"I know what to say," Kangata assured them. "I must go quickly to the other kraals and return in time to help Mdingi with the cows."

ELEVEN: # A Reward for Nomusa

Chief Zitu squatted on his special bamboo mat in the hut of his wife Makanya. He sniffed the food in the bowl Nomusa handed him.

"I think I know what meat this is," he said to his wife.

"It is Nomusa's wild boar," Makanya said, proudly.

"I have heard about it." Nomusa's father looked at her keenly. "It is a pity Nomusa is a girl, because she would have made a good hunter. I could use another strong, brave boy to help on this hunt."

"If I were allowed to go with you on the hunt, I might be able to catch another boar for you on the way," Nomusa suggested, surprised at her own daring.

"Nomusa! What are you saying!" reproved her mother.

But Zitu smiled good-naturedly and caught her arm in his powerful hand, feeling her hard little muscles. "Nomusa is strong—as strong as many boys older than she is. And she is clever and brave."

He looked at his daughter again, and then at his wife. "If Nomusa wishes, she may come on the hunt. But she must be sure to cause me no shame."

Nomusa's eyes widened with surprise. Makanya was speechless. "Oh, my father, thank you!" Nomusa burst out. "Please let me go with you, yes, yes!" She turned to her mother. "I know Sisiwe will do some of my work."

As if her father had already arranged everything, he declared, "Mdingi lost the cow, and you found her, so he will not go on the hunt this time. Kangata, of course, is too young. Between your brothers and Sisiwe, your mother will be able to get her work done." Zitu pushed away his bowl, saying, "I have finished."

Makanya handed him some white clay with which to remove the grease from his fingers. When Nomusa brought him the water gourd again, he rinsed his mouth and with his fingers rubbed the food from his teeth. He was clean again.

The business of the hunt settled, Zitu gave his attention to his wife and baby. Nomusa slipped quietly out of the hut.

She felt as if she would burst with joy and looked for someone to tell. Themba was standing outside the hut, looking lonely. To relieve her feelings, Nomusa picked him up, pulled his hair gently, and turned him upside down until his little pink heels wriggled in the air. Themba squealed with delight, and Dube hopped up and down, bewildered at this curious kind of play.

Sisiwe came along, bearing vegetables from her mother's garden.

"Oh, Sisiwe," Nomusa cried, "our father says I may go on the elephant hunt!"

Sisiwe was too surprised to say anything.

"Will you take care of Dube for me while I am gone?" Nomusa asked.

"Of course, my sister," Sisiwe answered. "And I will help your mother, too," she added generously. "Yo,

Nomusa, what do you think the other girls will say?"

There were no preparations to make for the trip, and the two days before the hunters were to meet were very long ones for Nomusa. She would have liked to talk about the hunt with her family. But she did not, because she saw Mdingi was hurt because she was going and he was not. Perhaps he really should be the one to go. Still, her father had said plainly that Mdingi would not be allowed to go, since he had lost the cow.

Timidly she spoke to Mdingi about her feelings. "I wish you were going on the hunt, my brother."

"It is no matter," Mdingi said indifferently.

But he was unhappy, Nomusa knew. How she wished there were something she could do to help him! If only Zitu knew how clever Mdingi was at composing songs and stories, how much he knew about birds and animals! And even so, he was a better shot with the bow and arrow than most of the boys. He had proved that at Damasi's party.

It was just that Mdingi did not care as a boy should for shooting and hunting and such things. Still, his pride was hurt when the chief chose his daughter to go with him on the elephant hunt instead of his son.

At dawn on the morning of the departure, Nomusa crept out of her hut very quietly, taking with her the empty water jar. She would leave everything in readiness for her mother when she awoke.

There would be just time enough to fetch the water, grind some mealie corn, and stir up the fire before it would be time to leave.

When she carried Dube over to Sisiwe's hut, he complained sleepily at being disturbed.

"It is going to be hard for me to leave you, little Dube," Nomusa said to him.

She fastened a cord to an outer post of Sisiwe's hut and attached the other end around Dube's neck. Then she gave him a bowl of *amasi,* which he dearly loved. Soon he began eating; the curds were too good to ignore.

While Dube ate, Nomusa looked in the direction of her father's hut to see if any of the hunters had yet arrived. She saw two glistening hunters entering through the kraal gate, their spears and large shields held close to their bodies. Nomusa left Dube abruptly and ran back to her hut. She had forgotten to get a handful of fat to rub on her body to make it glisten like the bodies of the other hunters. She had heard that fat made one active and supple.

Rubbing and polishing herself did not take long. Nomusa had done her work well, and she was ready to leave the hut. With a final glance to see that all was prepared for her mother when she awoke, she decided that she could now leave. She had just got outside without awakening any of her family when she heard an insistent call. "Nomusa, wait!"

Startled, she turned round and saw Mdingi with a bow and arrows in his hand. Her heart leaped. Had he determined to go and make her stay behind?

"What is it?" asked Nomusa.

"Here. Take these with you. You will need a good weapon," and he offered her the bow and arrows.

"They are your best bow and arrows!" exclaimed Nomusa, too surprised even to touch them.

"Ay, but I want you to have them. I am disappointed that I have to stay at home, but I am not angry with you."

Overcome by Mdingi's generosity, Nomusa did not know what to say. She hesitated to take the offered bow and arrows, but finally did so. "You are good, my brother. I am sorry it is not you who will use the bow and arrows. I shall take good care of them."

"It matters not about them. Only see to it that no harm comes to *you*," Mdingi said. "We shall be awaiting your return."

He touched her arm affectionately and ran to the cattle kraal without another word.

Off to the Hunt

Nomusa's father had already come out of his hut to greet the hunters who had coughed their notice of arrival. He was standing in front of his two tall neighbors, laughing and talking with them.

As Nomusa came up to her father, carrying Mdingi's bow and arrows, she politely said, *"Bayete!"*

Zitu said proudly, "Here is Nomusa my daughter." Then, looking at her with a twinkle in his eye, he added, "She will show us how to catch wild boars. She is an expert."

Those who were not going on the hunt were already awakened by the noise of the hunters; they hurried to stand a short distance off in order to watch what was going on. Although Themba could not see his sister, Nomusa could see him staring, wide-eyed, curious about all that was going on. More and more hunters arrived with their dogs, until there were about forty men and boys and a dozen dogs.

Nomusa heard one of the hunters saying, "I starved my dog three days to make him keen for this hunt."

"Ay," answered another, "mine is like a hyena. He has had no food for a long time, either. Are you sure the bitter bark you told me to chew on the morning of the hunt will strengthen my wind? So far I do not feel its benefit."

"Yo! It has never failed," said the first. "Look, over there. Someone is sweeping one of the huts. Bad luck! In our kraal, no one is allowed to sweep on the morning of the hunt, lest we return empty-handed."

The moment Nomusa heard this, she was filled with such dread at this bad omen that she crept out between the long black legs of the hunters, ran to Themba, and said, "Go quickly and tell Somcuba's sister that there must be no sweeping on the morning of the hunt, or we shall have bad luck."

Themba hurried off to carry out Nomusa's order.

Now that all the hunters had assembled, they formed little bands of relatives or close neighbors. First they began by saluting their chief, dancing before him. Each group danced and rushed around the kraal, yelling and boasting of their courage and strength. Then

they formed a huge circle around their chief and stood respectfully before him.

Nomusa's father began to instruct them as to their positions in the hunt. Every time he finished a sentence, the hunters would strike on the ground with their spears and shout, *"Tshilo!"*

Zitu said, "You all know the rules of the hunt, but in case anyone has forgotten, I shall tell you again that the first man to draw the blood of the prey is the owner. The next man to stab it can claim a leg, and if it is necessary for a third to strike, he may have a shoulder. The chief receives a leg from every animal." He looked around with a severe expression to see if everyone was paying attention, and continued. "If a small animal is killed, the hunter who has killed it must immediately carry it to me and claim it as his own. In this way there can be no quarrels. You have all heard?"

There were loud calls of *"Yo!"* *"Hau!"* "It is understood."

"We go now," said Nomusa's father.

A happy murmur rose through the crowd, accompanied by the clink of metal weapons as the hunters arranged their shields, spears, bows and arrows, and liana ropes. The journey began.

Nomusa could hardly believe they were really on their way. Filing out of the kraal close behind Zitu, she turned her head hastily to see if she could catch a last glimpse of Dube. Perhaps Sisiwe was in the crowd, holding the little monkey, but Nomusa's view was blocked by a solid wall of moving men. It was hopeless to try to see anything behind them.

As they marched along, the warming rays of the rising sun fell on the dew-soaked ground which looked so green and fresh. The wet grass swished damply against the hunters' naked bodies. Nomusa wondered what the elephant country would be like. Would it be as rolling, would there be as many narrow little streams, would there be wide meadows? Nomusa had never been further than Damasi's kraal on its flat-topped hill. She had often tried to imagine what the country might be like far beyond. That there were places where there were eland, lions, elephants, inyala, sassaby, and springbok she knew from having heard stories of previous hunts. She had heard that there was even a world of water called an ocean, if one kept walking east as far as one could go.

The hunters talked and laughed, now and then pointing to some indistinct moving object off in the far distance. Their curiosity and laughter were easily aroused. It interested Nomusa to see how playful these grown men were. They behaved no more seriously than her small brothers. Only her father remained dignified, walking ahead with a long stride, eyes alert, ears keen.

After Nomusa had walked behind him for some time, Zitu unexpectedly turned his head in her direction as if he had suddenly remembered that Nomusa was with them. He looked at her and said, "We have far to go. I hope you do not tire easily."

"That I do not," answered Nomusa, looking into Zitu's friendly eyes. At the moment it was difficult to imagine how fierce and angry he could be. Should she dare to ask him how far they were to walk before they reached elephant country? It would be useful to know, so that she would not be expecting to see elephants crash out at them all along the way. Not that she was afraid, but it was good to know what to expect.

"Come, Nomusa. Walk along beside me," suggested her father. "It will make it easier for you if you have anything to ask."

Quickly Nomusa ran forward, trying to match her step to his. She thought her father even slowed up a little so that she would not have to take little running steps to keep up with him.

"Is it far to the elephant country?" asked Nomusa.

"It is about five sleeps away," Zitu answered, his eyes on the path ahead. "It may be nearer or farther than that. Much depends on whether herds of elephants are moving south or north, and whether we walk along speedily and without any mishap. We are headed for some high country and wide rivers where elephants like to wander."

Nomusa listened carefully. That was just what she wanted to know. Proudly she walked, letting nothing escape her notice. Oh, there was a crested crane! She had never seen one before, but she knew what it was. "Look, Father!" urged Nomusa excitedly.

"Not good to eat," Zitu replied, indifferent.

Nomusa was about to say that she had pointed it

out for its beauty and not as something to eat, but she checked herself. Perhaps hunters should not think of things along the way except as a possibility for food or for exchange, like elephants' tusks.

She now walked along silently, thinking of the red bush lily she saw in one place, of the grassland flowers she saw in another. The farther they walked from the kind of country she was used to, the more different trees and wild flowers she saw. She must remember to tell Sisiwe about the gladioli she saw growing wild next to that narrow stream at which they stopped to drink. She would hardly believe it. And the birds! Even Mdingi had never seen so many. A flying hammerkopf attracted her attention as it snapped up frogs in a marshy pool.

After some distance, Nomusa saw her father wiping his perspiring brow with the back of his hand. "The sun is high," he declared. "In a little while we must stop to eat and rest until the sun's rays are not so hot."

When they reached a clear running stream, the chief turned and called to the hunters, "Here! A good place for eating and resting."

Immediately all came together, and as if they had

already agreed on what was to be done, some left to
go off into the woods to look for small animals, others
began gathering brushwood for a fire. Several took out
of a small sack some mealies and yams.

Nomusa looked at everything with the liveliest
interest. She quenched her thirst in the swiftly moving
stream and then hurried to help carry twigs and
branches to the blazing fire. Zabala, Damasi, and the
other boys did their share of the work, obeying the
orders of the older hunters.

Before long the hunters returned one by one with
rabbits, partridges, some quail, and a guinea hen, which
they set to cleaning and roasting.

As they waited for the food to cook, Nomusa
rested. Soon Damasi came to her, holding two half-
cooked partridge legs. "For you," he said, offering
Nomusa one.

When everyone had eaten, the hunters lay on the
grassy bank under the protecting shade of tall plane
trees. They rested or slept until Zitu gave the signal to
start off again.

Towards evening Nomusa felt so weary as she

trudged along that she could hardly wait for her father to call a halt. And though she did not like to admit it, even to herself, distant sounds of animals half frightened her. She heard the hoarse growl of a lion and barks she could not identify. Nomusa looked at the others, but they went on as if they had heard nothing. With the early moon climbing high over the horizon, there was still plenty of light to walk by so long as they kept to the open spaces. At last, however, it was necessary to stop, for a dark wood lay in front of them which the moon's rays could not penetrate. Zitu called a halt.

Now a very large fire was made. It would not be used only for cooking and warming purposes; it would have to last all through the night to keep away prowling animals, as well. Tonight there was no time for any of them to hunt for food, and they depended on what they still had in their sacks of mealies and yams. The food, though not plentiful, was filling; and when each had eaten his share, he lay down to sleep, close to the fire. Nomusa was glad to hear Zitu appoint one of the hunters as sentinel.

Nomusa was lying on her back looking up into the

star-studded sky, wondering how far they were from their kraal, when she saw something moving high up in the trees. Her heart thumped wildly. She was about to move over quietly to warn her father, when she saw the leaves stir again. A baboon! *Hau!* There was another, holding a baby. A baboon family was nesting in the tree.

Suddenly there was a muffled squeal as one of the mothers slapped her baby and grabbed it by the hair on the back of its head. Apparently it had put something in its mouth that it should not have. The mother baboon stuck her finger into the baby's mouth and pried out what it was eating. The howl from the baby caused dozing hunters to reach for their weapons. Then they saw the baboons, and one said, "They will not bother us if we do not bother them."

A loud bark came from the father baboon. He seemed to be scolding and saying, "Stop that awful noise!" The cries ceased, and all was still in the baboon family once more. Everything seemed safe and peaceful, and Nomusa fell asleep.

THIRTEEN: # An Unexpected Feast

The following morning the direction the hunters took led them toward high land. The air was gray and a little misty. Out of the mist Nomusa heard a voice calling out to her. It was Damasi's. His teeth flashed white as he smiled at Nomusa. They walked along side by side, saying little; the long climb made them both rather short of breath.

"It is a long way to the elephant country," Nomusa said at last.

"Yes," Damasi replied. "Some say five sleeps away, some say more."

By noonday they were high up in the hills. Below them they saw the rolling, grassy plains. The hot rays

of the sun were beginning to make the air before
Nomusa's eyes appear in crooked, glassy waves.

When the hunting party reached a waterfall that
cascaded over boulders to the rocks and plains below,
Zitu ordered a halt. Nomusa hoped it was so that they
might eat. She was not used to going without food for
such long periods. At home, when the children were
hungry, they ate. There was always enough.

While Nomusa and Damasi and the other boys
set to work finding dry twigs and branches with which
to start a fire, the older hunters cooled their perspiring
bodies under the waterfall. They laughed and enjoyed
themselves immensely, shouting and splashing each
other.

However, when they saw the fire well under way,
the men quickly came out from under the waterfall.
Taking their weapons they went to look for game.

Nomusa and Damasi and Zabala took their turn
under the splashing water. Emerging cool and refreshed,
they stood in the sun to dry their dripping bodies.

Nomusa was looking at the plain below when
something caught her eye. It looked like a black ball

and a brown ball moving horizontally across the sky-
line at great speed, apparently without touching the
earth. They became bigger, blacker, and browner as
they moved closer.

"Look, Damasi!" she cried. "What can that be?"

Damasi looked in the direction Nomusa pointed
to, puzzled for a moment. Then he said: "I know!
Ostriches! A male and a female. They must have been
frightened by something. They are galloping so fast we
cannot see their legs." Damasi looked at Nomusa,
laughing. "We might wish we could run as fast if some
wild animal were chasing us."

The barking of dogs heralded the return of the hunters. They had had good luck, and now everyone fell to cleaning and preparing the birds and animals for cooking. After the meal they slept. It seemed to Nomusa that she had barely lain down when there came urgent calls to get up and march on.

There was no time for an extra stretch or another wink. When her father said, "We go!" he meant it. The hunters had already extinguished the fire.

Toward evening they found themselves on a scrubby plain dotted with old thorn trees. Nomusa admired the reddened sky, flushed by the quick and beautiful sunset. The sunsets never failed to leave her astonished by the vivid coloring that faded swiftly into gray, then almost black. It was a marvel how quickly the sunset was over. Down went the sun into the mysterious horizon like a stone dropped in a pool.

The shadows became heavier and blacker. The hunters grew more watchful. This was the kind of country lions liked to roam.

Nomusa hoped her father would not decide to spend the night on this unpleasant-looking plain. She could not help feeling it was dangerous. But how much farther could they walk in the darkness? The dogs whined uneasily and drew close to their masters.

All at once the hunters who led the way stopped. There was a sudden hush, and the men held their weapons ready.

What was it that had stopped them? Nomusa looked up at her father questioningly, but he was too concerned with something under a large thorn tree to notice her. Zabala and Damasi, now boldly in front, were pointing at something very long and thick lying on the ground. It bulged in the middle, with two high knobs jutting under its flesh.

The object did not move. Whatever it was, it seemed to be dead. Now the hunters moved closer, step by step, holding back the excited dogs.

As they drew nearer, Nomusa saw that the object was a huge snake that had swallowed some small animal.

"The snake is dead," announced her father. "Let us cut him open and see what he has swallowed."

The snake was carefully cut open right around the part that bulged. There lay a young spotted deer, completely intact, that had apparently been swallowed not very long before. The two knobs under the snake's skin were the deer's budding horns.

Damasi came running over to Nomusa. "Do you see what has happened?" he asked excitedly. "The snake must have swallowed the young deer and then lain quietly down to digest it. When he fell asleep the horns of the deer ripped through his flesh and killed him. What a feast we shall have tonight!"

And what a fine story this is going to make for Themba, thought Nomusa.

"I have not tasted deer meat for a long time," said Damasi, smacking his lips.

"It is a pity that I am not as hungry now as I was at noonday," Nomusa sighed.

Zitu ordered an extra large fire to be made. Not far from the dead snake the hunters roasted the deer, pleased over their good luck in finding such a magnificent supper with so little effort. They gorged themselves with food as if they had not eaten for days, and even Nomusa could not resist the delicious smells of the roasting deer meat.

Sentinels were now appointed to watch over them while they slept, and a large crackling fire was kept burning to ward off any wild animals and to warm the hunters when the night grew cold. Nomusa did not enjoy having to sleep on this plain, especially as the dead snake was near enough to attract jackals or hyenas to their neighborhood.

She stared into the leaping flames, determined not to fall asleep. She would be a self-appointed sentinel tonight. Two would not be too many. But the warmth of the fire and her overburdened stomach conquered her determination to stay awake. Nomusa slept peacefully until sunrise the next morning.

FOURTEEN: Elephant Country

"Today we are in elephant country."
Zitu's words were loud enough for everyone to hear,
though he spoke to Nomusa, who was walking by his
side. "I expect we shall see elephant tracks before
sunset."

"You were right then, my father," Nomusa said
admiringly, "when you first told me the elephants were
five sleeps away."

"I have been here before—many times," the chief
replied. "Usually elephants stay in about the same
places. It was not any special wisdom on my part that
I should know this."

Nomusa was proud that her father, though an
important Zulu chief, never pretended to know more

than he actually did. She had heard of chiefs who claimed to have mysterious sources of knowledge and power, who were haughty and imperious with their people. Sometimes they were cruel, too. But not Zitu. He was simple and just. Although as chief he was entitled to a larger share of whatever came to them, he never took more than an ordinary Zulu.

Nomusa and her father were passing a grove of trees when she called: "See, over there! How strange those trees are! Why do they have no bark on them?"

Zitu looked where Nomusa pointed. It was as she said. There were trees without bark, or with large strips of it peeling off and hanging limply to the ground. Even the sides of some of the trees looked worn down.

"Yo! Elephants have been using this grove," exclaimed Zitu. "You have sharp eyes, my daughter." He looked keenly at the trees and the ground around them. Several of the smaller trees had been uprooted, and not a blade of grass remained. Nomusa saw the enormous footprints of the elephants in the soft earth.

"Hear me!" Zitu spoke in a very serious tone, and the hunters listened to him with respectful attention.

"Now that we are really in elephant country, we must be more cautious than ever before. Those of you who have never been on an elephant hunt do not know how dangerous it can be.

"A few years ago, Caluza, one of our bravest hunters, was killed and two others were badly wounded by an enraged elephant. We came upon a herd that had smelled us before we knew where they were. The first thing we heard was their furious trumpeting; then suddenly we saw them, waving their trunks and fanning out their great ears menacingly.

"With no further warning they charged us. We leaped to one side to throw our spears at the beasts. But one elephant seized Caluza with his trunk. He dashed him over and over against a tree until there was no life in him. Then he threw him down and trampled his body horribly."

Zitu paused, looking at the ring of faces. "We took back tusks from that hunt," he said slowly, "but we paid too dearly for them. Let us hope there will be no sorrow in the kraals when we return from this hunt.

"We must find the elephants before they find us.

And each one must do his part at just the right time. One more thing: we must not kill an elephant too close to the river, for then he will fall in the water and we shall never get the tusks.

"Use your eyes and use your ears! We go now."

As they started Zabala came running to his father. "Look over here!"

Zabala had found the path by which the elephants entered and left the grove. It was smooth and hard; they must have used it many times.

"These tracks are not fresh. I think it is many days since the elephants visited this grove," said one of the hunters. "The droppings look old."

"Let us go in that direction," Zitu decided, pointing the way. "And quietly. Hold your weapons ready but do not use them until I give the signal."

As they moved along the path, Nomusa wondered how many elephants they would find at one time, how they would manage to get an elephant back to their kraal, how she would succeed in hitting an elephant with Mdingi's arrow in just the right spot to kill it. Her mind was so full of these thoughts that she did not look carefully in front of her. All at once she stepped on a bunch of dry twigs, making such a loud snapping noise that the hunters were startled. They turned angrily, frowning at Nomusa.

Zitu said quietly: "We do not want anyone to say that this is what happens when we take a girl along. Such a noise might drive the elephants at us or away from us entirely. Let them but smell or hear us and things might go badly! One person's carelessness can endanger us all. Do not let it happen again."

As if her father had to tell her that! Nomusa was overwhelmed by her feeling of disgrace. Zitu would know better than to take a girl with him another time.

On went the hunters, paying no further attention to Nomusa. She walked along in their midst, her eyes fast to the ground, still filled with shame. After a while she felt a gentle nudge at her elbow. At first she paid no attention to it, thinking one of the hunters had accidentally bumped her. But when the nudge became more insistent, she looked up and saw Damasi. He grinned sympathetically and offered her some wild figs.

Nomusa felt too unhappy to take any, and she

solemnly shook her head in refusal. Damasi did not
press her, but began eating them himself. They continued walking side by side for some time. Then
Nomusa turned her head to see if Damasi had left any
figs for her. He caught her glance and rubbed his
middle enthusiastically to show how good the figs had
been. He held out an empty hand and pointed down
his throat to show where the plump figs had gone.

Nomusa's disappointed look amused Damasi, and
he could not help laughing. She decided that he was a
greedy boy, no different from all the others.

But soon Damasi nudged her again and teasingly
showed her the same handful of figs he had held out
to her the first time. Despite herself, Nomusa smiled.
Damasi had only pretended he had eaten them. This
time she did not risk refusing the figs, but took them
eagerly. She gave back half to Damasi, and together
they walked on, eating cheerfully. By now Nomusa had
forgotten her disgrace, but she did not forget to be careful.

Just before noon, the elephant path they were
following disappeared into the grassy plains.

"This is the time to take greatest care," Zitu said,

and the word was passed quietly among the hunters. They moved slowly and noiselessly, searching for new elephant tracks.

As they approached a wide deep river, they heard loud splashing sounds. The hunters stood still for a moment, listening; then they moved on silently toward the river.

As they drew closer, the splashing sound grew louder. Their view of the water was hidden by what looked like a wall of large, light blue butterflies, hundreds and hundreds of them, fluttering up and down all the way from the ground to a height taller than the tallest hunter.

The chief signaled to the hunters to creep behind some bushes so they would not have to part the butterfly wall to see the river. As she came noiselessly from behind the bushes, Nomusa was surprised and delighted to see a mother elephant pushing her baby elephant into the water for a bath. The baby did not want to go in, but the determined mother was shoving it into the river with her trunk.

In the meantime, the father elephant, quite unconcerned, was giving himself a shower bath by sucking up great quantities of water through his trunk and then squirting it—*swooshh!*—over his back. Again and again the huge bull elephant did this. He was having a wonderful time. The corners of his mouth were pulled back, and his eyes were partly closed as he sprayed the water over his massive head.

The cow elephant finally succeeded in pushing her baby into the water, and she blew a shower of water over it. The little one tried to escape by scrambling up the bank. Some of the hunters raised their spears, prepared to hurl them as soon as their chief gave the sign.

But Zitu signaled the hunters not to throw their spears at the elephants. Nomusa was surprised, and strangely happy, too. The chief pointed to the elephant tusks and showed with his hands that they were too small. Now Nomusa understood. They had not come to hunt elephants just to kill them, but to obtain the largest tusks possible. She remembered now that she had heard that white traders were very glad to get large elephant tusks and that good exchanges were made for them.

The little elephant seemed very content to be in the water now, and he splashed and spluttered as much as his father and mother. In a mischievous moment, the baby sucked up a great trunkful of water and blew it full in his father's face. Astonished and irritated, the bull elephant rushed at his disrespectful offspring. He pushed him into such deep water that he lost his foothold.

Frightened, the little elephant lifted his short trunk

into the air and trumpeted frantically while he swam
to shallower water. At last he scrambled safely to shore.
He had learned how to behave toward his father.

The hunters moved on until they were far from
the river scene. Then they stopped to eat.

They rested for a while; then Zitu rose. "We must
be on our way. We are in the neighborhood of elephants, and I do not want to spend the night in their
midst without locating some with good tusks."

After they had walked for some distance, Zitu
stood still, listening. The men stopped, waiting for their
chief's decision. In the dismal hush different calls of
forest birds could be heard, mingled with an occasional
howl from some animal. Then faintly there came to
their ears the sound of low rumblings and gurglings.
Nomusa pointed urgently in the direction from which
the sound had come. Her father nodded, now smiling.
He had heard too, and so had all the others.

Very, very carefully they moved in the direction
of the sound, weapons ready. While they crept closer,
stopping from time to time in order to keep away from
the wind side, Zabala's arm suddenly waved up and

down in a frenzy as he saw something moving between two tall trees. A large ear could be seen flapping slowly. Yo! They had come upon a herd of elephants feeding. The hunters stood stock-still, their eyes wide with excitement.

When Zitu decided which elephants they would attack, he pointed out to each of his men what position to take. Nomusa wormed her way forward after Zabala and Damasi. She peeped through the screen of leaves to see the enormous creatures whose ears seemed to flap among the topmost branches of the trees.

Eight elephants were in the clearing, three of them bulls, four cow elephants, and one baby elephant, a very small one indeed. Nomusa drew back stealthily and held up eight fingers to show her father how many elephants she had seen. The hunters nodded their heads, well pleased with the information.

Zitu crept forward and peered through the bushes. He had to find out which elephants had the best tusks. Nomusa looked again when her father did, and now she saw a sight that delighted her. The baby elephant was under her mother, trying to suck some milk from her while the mother was grazing. The mother elephant kept pushing the little one out from under her, but her persistent baby would not stay away.

It amazed Nomusa to see the size of the bulls. They were huge, bigger than anything she had ever seen. While they ate, their stomachs rumbled, and they slobbered with their mouths and ground their teeth. None of the beasts ever seemed to stand still. They were constantly moving and shifting their feet, flapping their great ears.

Two of the bull elephants had especially large, heavy tusks. These were the ones Zitu pointed out to

his men. They got into positions from which they could get a better view of the herd and a closer aim. Unless they hit the elephants in exactly the right spot, they would not be able to kill them. Nomusa knew that a wounded elephant is a ferocious beast. These next few moments would be extremely dangerous ones. Her heart began to pound so hard she was afraid the elephants would hear it.

The chief now made a quick sign. With all their strength and skill the hunters hurled their sharp-pointed spears at the two bull elephants. Nomusa's bow twanged as she let her arrow fly, aiming for the vulnerable spot under the elephant's ear. Zabala and Damasi hurled their short spears.

A great uproar set up among the elephants. Trumpeting and screaming, their heads up and tails held out stiffly, they charged the bushes where the hunters lay hidden.

Suddenly there was a great thud, and unexpectedly the herd turned in the opposite direction and thundered off. After a moment the hunters crept out of their hiding place to see what had happened.

One of the huge bull elephants lay on its side, a mountain of flesh enclosed in a gray wrinkled skin. Nomusa and the others stared at the enormous mass, hardly able to believe they had killed this giant.

"We were very lucky," said Zitu. "I think I know what happened. As the herd charged at us, this one fell dead in its path. That turned the others."

The chief rubbed his hand along the handsome tusks of the dead elephant. "They are fine tusks."

In the meantime Nomusa and Damasi had been looking at the path made by the herd as they rushed off. Small trees had been uprooted and great branches broken off others. Nomusa stared at the ground.

"Look!" she cried. "A trail of blood!"

"The other elephant must have been very badly wounded," Zitu said, crouching down to examine the tracks.

He stood up, looking at the sun. "It grows late," he said, concern in his voice. "But if we do not find the wounded bull today, we may never do so.

"We must follow him now," the chief decided; and he led the way.

FIFTEEN: # A Wounded Bull

The trail of blood was easy to follow at first, but it was not very long before Nomusa understood why Zitu was worried. The sun was sinking deeper and deeper, and Nomusa remembered how quickly darkness came after sunset.

From time to time they came to large patches of flattened grass where the wounded elephant had fallen, to rise again and move on.

The hunters kept their eyes on the ground, and their ears were keenly alert to all the sounds about them. They knew how dangerous a wounded bull elephant could be, and other fierce animals might be prowling.

It became more and more difficult to see the trail of the animal, and Nomusa began to fear night would fall before they found him.

Then Sihkulumi, one of the hunters in the lead, stopped dead in his tracks, pointing.

"Hau!" he said. "There he is!"

Ahead of them they saw the wounded elephant lying against a tree that seemed to bend with his huge weight.

"He is dead!" Sihkulumi cried, and he rushed forward. Zitu spoke a restraining word; then he raced after Sihkulumi.

Even as the hunter reached him, the elephant heaved his huge bulk upright. His trunk shot out, enveloping Sihkulumi. He would surely be killed, crushed to death by the powerful trunk.

Nomusa saw her father, fearfully close to the elephant, taking sure aim. Then his bow twanged, and the arrow sped to the elephant's brain.

The beast dropped dead, and Sihkulumi's body fell to the ground. Zitu was beside him in a moment. Soon Sihkulumi sat up, not hurt, only shaken and frightened. But he could not look at the chief, and when he spoke his voice was full of shame.

"I was not worth risking your life for," he said. "If I had remembered to wait for your orders, there would have been no danger."

Zitu helped him to his feet. "I am thankful that you are alive," he said simply. "I believe you will never be foolish again."

He turned to the others. "We shall stay here tonight. We shall need a very large fire to frighten away animals."

Nomusa went about gathering wood with the others, but she could not forget the sight of Zitu as he faced the elephant. This was a story that would be told about the evening fires for many moons.

The hunters cut off great chunks of elephant meat to roast over the fire. What a feast they had! Nomusa was surprised to discover how good the meat tasted. But it was very tough to chew. When everyone had eaten as much as he wanted, Zitu chose the first sentry for the night, and all lay down to sleep.

What animals howled or roared through the

night, only the sentinels knew. Nomusa and the other weary hunters were awakened at dawn the next morning, greeted by the smell of roasting elephant meat.

In the morning the men started the difficult task of cutting the huge tusks out of the elephant's jaw. It took hours and hours. But at last they were out and lying side by side on the ground, where everyone admired their size and beauty. Then Zitu appointed two men to carry each tusk. "Everyone take turns," the chief said.

As they marched, Nomusa began to feel very tired and thirsty. Her head ached and throbbed, and although the day was not hot, she felt as if she were burning. And how unbearably thirsty she was!

Insect bites and sores on her body which she had received along the way, and to which she had paid little attention, now seemed very troublesome. Still, she was determined that she would not make Zitu regret taking her on this hunt. Not a word would she say about being thirsty and tired. But she had lost interest in elephants and in anything that was to be seen along the trail. Her only thought was of her longing for water and a place to lie down. How she wished she were with her mother. Makanya would be sure to know what to do to make her feel better.

Finally Nomusa could go no farther. She would have to stop no matter what happened. The others could go on without her.

Nomusa lay down on a grassy slope, hidden by the long grass. She closed her eyes. The hunters filed past without knowing she was lying there. How long she lay there Nomusa did not know. She must have fallen asleep.

She lay like a stone on the earth; then she became dimly aware of someone bending over her and saying, "Are you sick, Nomusa?" The voice sounded far away.

Nomusa opened her eyes. "Oh, Damasi," she said weakly, "I am very tired, and so thirsty."

"We have come to a little stream, not far from here, where we are all bathing and resting. Come," he urged.

"You were good to come back for me," murmured Nomusa.

"It was not I who thought of it first," admitted

Damasi. "While we were sitting at the stream your father suddenly missed you and asked me to go back and look for you. Let us go. I shall help you."

When they came to the hunters, Damasi took Nomusa directly to her father. "Sit here," Zitu said. "Damasi, bring water."

Out of a pouch in his belt Zitu took some powdered herbs, which he mixed with water. It was a bitter drink, and Nomusa shuddered as she swallowed it.

"Now rest," her father said gently.

As she drank more water Nomusa began to grow comfortably warm, and her cold sweat turned to warm perspiration. "Ah, that is well," said her father as he felt her brow. "You will feel better now. I think you did not chew the elephant meat well enough. The first time I ate elephant meat I felt ill, too." It comforted Nomusa to hear this.

Before long Nomusa felt quite strong again; she was ready to get up and go along. When Zitu saw this, he gave the signal to start.

"It is not very far from here where we left the first elephant," he said.

Nomusa kept a sharp lookout, hoping to be the first to see it. But it was Zitu's keen eyes that found the animal. The chief stopped, frowning.

"*Hau!*" he cried. "What is this?"

There, swarming over the elephant like black ants, were many tiny dark people. Who were they and what were they doing on her father's elephant? Nomusa

wondered. There would certainly be trouble now. Nomusa saw the faces of her father and the other hunters fill with anger. Chief Zitu shouted, "We killed this elephant! It belongs to us!"

The small people answered in a storm of words none of the Zulus understood. Threateningly they picked up their toylike bows and arrows. The Zulu hunters raised their spears, ready to use them at a word from their chief. Nomusa was excited and afraid too. There would surely be a terrible fight.

But Zitu spoke to them again, in a quieter tone. He made signs with his hands, saying that he and his men must have the tusks, but the little people could have the rest of the elephant. At last they understood, and they laid down their weapons, to the great relief of all. The Zulus, too, dropped their weapons on the ground and slowly approached the dead elephant.

The small people began cutting open the huge animal. As Nomusa watched, she saw how carefully they pulled out the eyelashes and the long hairs from the elephant's ears. They seemed to treasure these especially. Some of them were cutting off chunks of elephant meat and eating it raw. How sick they will be! thought Nomusa.

Full of curiosity about these small people, Nomusa drew near her father and asked, "My father, who are these strange people? They do not seem at all like us."

"They are Pygmies, who live in the forest here," Zitu replied. "Only once before have I ever met any, and that was when we had gone on a hunt ten sleeps away. These Pygmies have wandered a long distance from their home, far to the north."

Nomusa kept her eyes fixed on the fascinating little people. She noticed that the tallest among them was just a little taller than she was. They were lighter in color than the Zulus, and much hairier.

While the hunters were hacking out the elephant's tusks, Nomusa stayed close to the Pygmies so she could learn as much as possible about them. They wore nothing but a small flap of eland skin below their fat bellies and had no ornaments of any kind. To Nomusa they looked very drab and bare without beads or bracelets. Their arms seemed too long for their bodies; their legs were short; their feet were very large. But their toes were the most remarkable of all. They were so long that they looked more like fingers than toes. How wonderful they must be for climbing trees! thought Nomusa.

The Pygmies moved quickly and seemed to have a natural cleverness in doing things. Nomusa felt much attracted to the little people when she saw how merry and playful they were, how helpful and kind to each other.

Some of them had made a fire and were smoking large chunks of elephant meat on pointed sticks. Others crawled inside the elephant and cut out the heart and liver, handing them to others on the outside.

After a while Nomusa noticed that from time to time a few Pygmies would disappear into the forest, carrying smoked meat on long sticks. She wondered where they went. Perhaps her father would let her follow them.

But this was no time to ask for a favor. Zitu was busy, and he did not like working with so many Pygmies swarming about him. They got in his way so that it was difficult to move without bumping into one of them. The little people were as curious about the Zulus as Nomusa was about the Pygmies.

When she saw her father looking more cheerful, Nomusa went to him and said, "My father, I am very curious about these small people and how they live. May I follow one of them when he goes into the forest?"

Zitu was silent for a moment, and Nomusa thought he was angry at her foolish request. But he only turned his head and called: "Sikhulumi! Come!"

Sikhulumi came quickly, and Zitu said: "My daughter wants to see where the Pygmies live. Go with her and look after her. You know a little of their language."

Sikhulumi nodded gravely. The tall hunter was pleased and proud that the chief entrusted him with such an errand, especially after his recklessness of the day before.

Zitu added, smiling: "Nomusa seems very much interested in these little people. Perhaps you can find her a husband among them."

Sikhulumi laughed, and Nomusa made a face.

As one of the Pygmies started off with a load, Zitu

tapped his shoulder. Smiling, he pointed to Nomusa. The Pygmy grinned, looking at Nomusa with great interest; but they could see he did not understand what was meant. Sikhulumi said a few words in the Pygmy language. The Pygmy finally smiled and nodded his head. He would guide them to the place where his people lived.

SIXTEEN: The Pygmy Settlement

Nomusa and Sikhulumi followed the little man through the dense forest. He walked swiftly and quietly, half running through bushes and under low branches. There was no path, and Nomusa and Sikhulumi had to move quickly to keep the Pygmy in sight. If they lost him, they might not easily find their way back to the hunters, much less find the Pygmy settlement.

Now and then the Pygmy turned to see if they were still following. Sometimes he slowed down to allow them to catch up with him. He was much stronger than he looked. Although he carried a heavy load of meat, he did not stop to rest even once.

At last they came to the Pygmy settlement. When

the other Pygmies saw Nomusa and Sikhulumi, they
stopped, looking startled. Nomusa's Pygmy companion
said something to them, pointing to the visitors. Then
the Pygmies came forward and helped carry the smoked
meat to one of their little houses.

Nomusa saw that these huts were made of bent
branches tied together with vines. Leaves were laid
over the branches to keep out the sun and rain. The
huts were small and not carefully made. Perhaps the
Pygmies did not bother to make a better hut because
they did not stay in one place very long. The Zulu huts
were much larger and stronger, for they stayed in the
same place for years and years.

Sikhulumi explained to Nomusa that the Pygmies
lived only on what wild animals they could catch and
on roots and berries found growing in the forest. The
Zulus owned cattle, and they planted their own gardens
with a wide variety of vegetables and fruits. They did
not have to wander from place to place in search of
food like the Pygmies.

Their Pygmy guide now invited them to come and
see the inside of a hut. Sikhulumi decided he was too

big to enter, but he urged Nomusa to go in. When she crawled in through the low opening, she saw a woman, smaller than herself, carrying a baby astride her hip. The woman was cooking something in a black pot over a fire. From time to time she left the hut, returning quickly with caterpillars or winged ants, snails or lizards. All these she threw into the pot. Once a small boy, little more than half the size of Themba, came in with a bush rat to put into the pot.

Nomusa observed that these people did not sleep on mats, but on dried skins of animals, or on leaves. The hut was empty, except for a few gourds. How different were the Zulu huts, thought Nomusa. Since her people stayed a long time in one place, it did not matter how many things they collected and kept in their huts. To people like the Pygmies, who moved often, it was important not to have many things to carry.

When Nomusa came out of the hut, she found Sikhulumi talking to a Pygmy who knew something of the Zulu language. He was asking Sikhulumi if he had any salt.

Sikhulumi shook his head regretfully. "If we come

next year, we will surely bring some," he promised.

The Pygmy seemed delighted with Nomusa. He asked her, "Are you married?"

Nomusa giggled. "No, I am only ten years old."

The man looked surprised. He came close to Nomusa and measured himself against her. He was only a tiny bit taller than she was. As he stood there Nomusa looked with interest at a necklace he wore. As she looked, she realized what it was. Now she knew why the Pygmies saved the elephant's eyelashes.

The Pygmy saw her interest in the elephant-hair necklace and quickly took it off and offered it to her. "Bring good luck," he said.

Nomusa looked at Sikhulumi.

"Take it," he advised. "You will have something very unusual to show your brothers and sisters."

Sikhulumi turned to the Pygmy. "How do your people kill elephants?"

"Come," said the little man. "I will show you."

The Pygmy brought out bows and arrows as well as slender spears so small that Nomusa thought little Themba would have been able to use them.

Nomusa saw that the tiny arrows were made of straight twigs of hardwood cut from a bush. The ends of the arrows were slit and a green leaf was stuck in each, instead of a feather such as the Zulus used.

The man pointed to the tips of the arrows and spears, saying, "Poison!"

"Where do you get the poison?" Nomusa asked.

The Pygmy explained. His people searched for poisonous herbs as well as for poisonous barks of trees. They also got poison from a certain black ant whose bite was terribly painful.

With many gestures, the Pygmy explained how they climbed trees under which they expected elephants to pass on their way to feeding grounds. The men in the trees threw down their poisoned spears on the passing elephants. while Pygmies on the ground shot poisoned arrows at the animals.

If the elephant did not die at once, the Pygmies knew that some of the poison would finally work inside the animal's body and kill him. They would follow him until he dropped. Usually, he assured them, they did not have long to wait.

Nomusa was still full of curiosity. "Do the boys take care of the cattle as my brothers do?"

The Pygmy looked surprised. "We have no cattle," he said. "We live by hunting."

"How long have you been living here?"

"Two moons. Soon we leave. More fruit, berries, tortoises, and monkeys in new place."

Nomusa suddenly remembered Dube. "You like monkeys?" she asked hopefully.

"Ay, very good to eat!"

It was time to go. Many of the small people came to look at the visitors curiously. Nomusa noticed that, like the men, the women wore no ornaments, beads, or bracelets.

Nomusa had a final question for the Pygmy. "How many wives do Pygmy men have?"

He looked shocked, then amused. "How many? One, of course."

Now Nomusa really felt sorry for these people. She realized how very poor the Pygmies were, for among the Zulus it was only a poor man who had but one wife.

Their guide was ready to take them back to their camp. The Pygmies waved a friendly farewell to their visitors. One woman gave Nomusa a present—a huge dried beetle, the largest Nomusa had ever seen.

With no load to carry, the Pygmy guide sped

through the forest so quickly that Nomusa and Sikhu-lumi had to run to keep up with him. He no longer bothered to look back to see if they were following. Perhaps he thought that anyone who had been over the ground once would surely know it again.

It was close to sundown, and when the long purple shadows of the trees fell across the ground, it became increasingly difficult to see the Pygmy.

At last what they feared had happened. Sikhulumi stopped, completely confused. Nomusa needed no word from him to tell her they were lost. The Pygmy was nowhere to be seen, and they did not know which path to take. Sihkulumi looked very anxious. Then they heard a whistle.

"It is he!" cried Nomusa. "But where?"

Where, indeed? Sihkulumi looked all about him. Then the whistle sounded again, and Sihkulumi's dark face broke into a grin. He raised his eyes to the high branches of a tree. There was the Pygmy, his small body barely discernible among the green leaves.

Down he scampered, agile as a monkey. In his hand was a big piece of honeycomb, some of which he gave to Nomusa and Sihkulumi. They walked along more slowly now, and together, eating the delicious honey. But Nomusa kept a watchful eye on the Pygmy. Perhaps he might decide to play another joke on them.

But they soon reached the others, without any difficulty. The Pygmies were still smoking elephant meat, but the Zulu hunters had finished their work. They squatted about the huge fire, resting and eating. Nomusa and Sihkulumi were glad to dip their fingers into the food pot, too.

As they ate and rested, Zitu spoke.

"We can be thankful that we have had a safe and successful hunt. Tomorrow at sunrise we set out for our kraals. Let everyone remember to take care along the way so that we shall have no mishap."

Growing drowsy by the fire, Nomusa thought of all the wonderful stories she had to tell Themba. And Mdingi would be sure to make good songs about many of the things Nomusa would tell him. Yo! She was every bit as eager to get home as she had been to leave!

Everyone was getting ready to sleep, and a sentinel had been appointed. Nomusa looked over at the

Pygmies to see what they were doing. The night had grown chilly, and the little men were beating their bodies with their hands and huddling close to the fire. Nomusa saw some Pygmies crawl inside the elephant. She expected them to come right out again. But they did not, and after a bit Nomusa went over to see why they stayed so long.

Inside the elephant the Pygmies lay, one next to the other, fast asleep.

SEVENTEEN: The Leopard in the Pit

On the homeward trip Nomusa kept watching for interesting birds and animals. She could never have too many stories to tell Themba and Umpondo and the other little brothers and sisters.

When they were about a day's journey from the kraals, the party rested on a flat-topped hill. Looking down on the valley, Nomusa beheld a wonderful sight. A number of lions, lionesses, and cubs lay among the tall grasses. The older animals seemed to be drowsing in the sun, but the cubs refused to stay quiet. Like kittens they played together, tumbling about, nipping each other's ears and tails.

How gentle they looked, Nomusa thought, even harmless. But she was glad to know they were far below her and the other hunters.

A small antelope appeared, a short distance away. the lions ignored it; this was not the time for hunting. But the lionesses growled, and their tails began to switch. The cubs looked at the antelope, and back at their mothers. The lionesses rushed forward with low growls, encouraging their frolicking cubs to come along.

"Look!" said Damasi, who sat watching beside Nomusa. "I think the lionesses are going to use the little antelope to teach the cubs how to hunt!"

A lioness kept the antelope at bay, while the cubs worried it. Sometimes the mother let the antelope run away, in order to see if the cubs could catch it by themselves. When they could not, she ran it down herself and pinned it to the ground; then she left the animal to the cubs.

One cub did not know what to do and ran wildly about the antelope, nipping its tail playfully. The mother rushed at her cub and smacked him with her

paw as if to tell him to behave like a lion and not like
a baby.

Nomusa would like to have watched more, but
again the Zulus were on the march. They were in a
hurry to get home, and they rested only briefly.

In the distance they could see the rolling hills on
which the kraals were situated. Nomusa was glad that
this was so, for she was very tired. How good it would
be to lie on her mat and sleep and sleep!

She was not keeping up with the others very well,
but no one seemed to pay any attention. Ahead of her

she could see Damasi walking with Zabala. They were having a good time laughing and talking together, and Nomusa thought crossly that Damasi seemed to have forgotten she was with them. He did not even look back to see where she was.

As she moved wearily along, Nomusa kept on thinking of the joy of returning. How glad she would be to see her mother and the baby sister! How she would hug her chubby little brother! And Mdingi and funny Kangata—

Nomusa's busy thoughts made her forget her weariness, but they made her less cautious, too. If she had been intent on where she was walking, she would have been suspicious of the place in the trail where some branches had fallen and the grasses were oddly disturbed. She would have gone around it as the others had.

But Nomusa's thoughts were far away, and the next thing she knew she lay at the bottom of a pit, on top of the body of a small leopard. It was dead, with an arrow in its neck. Her first feeling was that she was thankful the leopard was dead. But soon she realized that she could not get out of the pit without help. In a frenzy she began shouting for someone to come and help her. How long must she stay here? Would she ever get out? The hunters might even reach the kraals before they knew she was missing.

Nomusa was brave, but it was dark and hot in the pit, and she was very tired. The minutes crawled by, and she began to feel less and less a fearless hunter and more and more a frightened ten-year-old girl.

Maybe she would never see her mother and her brothers and sisters again. Maybe they would never find her and never know what had happened to her. Tears welled up in Nomusa's eyes in spite of herself. Again she called, this time somewhat feebly. Thirst consumed her, and her body felt unbearably hot and sticky. Why, oh why, had she ever wanted to be a hunter? If only she had stayed at home this would never have happened to her.

She tried several times to make toeholds in the sheer sides of the pit, but the soft earth crumbled away. By now she didn't even know what time of day it was. It seemed ages since she had fallen into the pit. She shuddered fearfully at the thought of being there all night. A live animal might fall in, too; Nomusa's vivid imagination pictured all sorts of dreadful encounters with snarling, clawing lions and leopards.

Again she called out in desperation. And, miracle of miracles! she heard an answering cry. She was sure it was Damasi's voice. "Nomusa! Where are you?"

"Here!" she shrieked. "In the pit! Be careful!"

The leaves and branches were parted, and there was Damasi looking down at her. Zabala was beside him.

"Yo! What a scare you gave us!" Zabala cried.

"Are you all right?" Damasi asked anxiously.

"Yes," said Nomusa, weakly. "But how frightened I have been!" she confessed.

"Who would not have been frightened?" Damasi answered, looking awesomely at the pit.

"How shall we get her out?" asked Zabala, practically.

Damasi considered. For once, Nomusa had no ideas. She was content to wait to be rescued.

"We must get strong vines and weave them together," Damasi decided. "Then Nomusa can attach them to herself and we can pull her out."

"You will need more than one," Nomusa said. "I have something here that I must bring up."

"What is that?" Zabala inquired.

"You shall see," Nomusa said mysteriously.

Before long Damasi threw down two lengths of woven vines. Nomusa tested them and found them

strong. One she bound securely about the leopard; the other she knotted under her arms. "Ready!" she called.

Zabala and Damasi braced themselves firmly and pulled with all their might. Nomusa held on tightly and dug her toes into the sides of the pit. Right now she wished they were long like the Pygmy's!

At last she was over the top of the pit and lay on the ground breathing hard. Damasi and Zabala looked at her with concern, touching her to be sure she was all right.

"Now the other," Nomusa said, finally, still panting.

This time the pull was easier, for there were three of them. Nomusa could not wait to see their faces when the leopard appeared.

"*Hau!*" the boys cried at the same time. "A leopard!"

They were still exclaiming over the handsome beast when Zitu and Sihkulumi and another hunter came running up. How relieved her father was to see Nomusa!

When he heard what had happened, Zitu looked at Zabala and Damasi proudly.

"You have done well," the chief said. "No man could have done better."

Nomusa looked timidly at her father. "I am sorry, my father. My carelessness has caused you much trouble."

Zitu nodded. "Some of the fault was yours," he agreed. "But I am to blame, too. In my eagerness to return home I did not look for you as I should have. Come," Zitu added gently. "We shall stop for the

night when we reach the others. It is too late to go on."

He directed the men to tie the leopard's legs to their spears and carry him back to the camp.

"The beast is yours," her father said to Nomusa. "You may do what you want with him."

Nomusa's heart was so full of joy and relief that she forgot her weariness. How wonderful to be free to walk again! And her father was not angry with her. Surely no girl ever had so much to be thankful for.

EIGHTEEN: # The Song Of Mdingi

As the hunters approached the kraal, those who had remained behind rushed out to meet them. The four huge ivory tusks were exclaimed over and admired.

"These are the finest tusks I have ever seen," said an old man, touching them with his hand. "They will be worth much in exchange."

Nomusa ran forward to greet her mother and to hug Themba joyously and dance him up and down.

"What stories I have to tell you, Themba! And here is a present for you," Nomusa added, putting the large beetle the Pygmy woman had given her into his fat little hands.

Sisiwe squeezed through the crowds, carrying Dube on her shoulder. The little monkey looked frightened at the crowds of people and the noise. Had he forgotten her, Nomusa wondered? She greeted Sisiwe affectionately and then spoke to Dube.

At the sound of her voice, Dube was all aquiver. When he saw her he strained forward. With one leap he was in Nomusa's arms, chattering "Tchirk? Tchirk?" as if to ask her why she had stayed away so long.

"He still loves you best," Sisiwe said, a little sadly.

"But you may play with him as often as you want," Nomusa said. "I shall not forget what good care you have taken of him, my sister."

Nomusa soon realized that she was indeed at home, for she heard her mother calling from their hut. "Nomusa! Fetch water!"

As she walked to the stream she was followed by a crowd of girls, all suddenly having to fetch water for their mothers. Nomusa was kept busy answering dozens of questions. The girls were especially interested in hearing about the Pygmies, and they laughed up-

roariously when Nomusa told about the Pygmy who had asked her if she was married.

It took much longer than usual to fetch water on this exciting day. By the time they returned, everyone was busy preparing for the evening feast in celebration of the successful hunt and the safe return of the hunters.

A huge stack of brushwood was being piled up outside the kraal to make a fire. Over this fire a bullock would be roasted, together with mealie cobs. Soon Nomusa's brothers began returning from the pasture with their mothers' cows. They had to return earlier today to help with the preparations for the evening.

Nomusa rushed to greet her brothers. "Oh, Mdingi, Kangata, how much I have to tell you! Put the cows in the cattlefold and hurry back!"

Soon her brothers sat beside Nomusa while she told about the snake that had swallowed the spotted deer, the fascinating Pygmies, the lions she had seen, and finally of her adventure in the pit. Her brothers listened, spellbound.

"Think if the leopard had been alive!" Kangata said, frightened at the very thought.

Nomusa smiled at him. "Here is a present for you, Kangata," she said. "The Pygmy told me this elephant-hair necklace would bring the wearer good luck."

Kangata put on the necklace, marveling at Nomusa's generosity. Mdingi rose.

"Your stories are exciting, my sister," he said. "I want to hear more soon. But now I must milk our mother's cows."

"Wait—come with me to the hut first," Nomusa said. "I have something for you, too."

When they got to the hut, Nomusa picked up the leopard skin, which she had asked Sihkulumi to remove carefully for her. She handed it to Mdingi.

The skin was a very beautiful one, and Mdingi was speechless with happiness.

"It is too much," he managed to say, finally.

"I am happy to give it to you," Nomusa answered softly. She was very glad it pleased him so much, because she knew how sad he had felt about not going on the elephant hunt.

Mdingi continued to gaze at his treasure and feel it with his fingers.

"I have another present for you," Nomusa added. "It is a different kind of present, but maybe you can use it." She told him the story of the wounded elephant that had attacked Sihkulumi and of their father's courage and daring.

"If I could make songs, like you," Nomusa said to her brother, "I should make a great song about this."

Mdingi's face had a kind of shining look that Nomusa had seen before. She thought he was seeing in his mind the heroic scene Nomusa had described to him, and the words of a song were already clamoring to be spoken.

Mdingi turned to go, clutching the leopard skin to him. "Thank you, Nomusa!" he said. "Thank you, thank you!"

The African moon shone big and full and yellow. The outlines of trees were dark against the sky, and the leaping flames of the fire danced higher and higher.

The people had eaten and drunk all they could hold, and now they sat in a great circle around the fire, listening as different singers chanted stories about the great Zulu hunters and warriors. Most of the stories had been told over and over, but the people always wanted to hear them again.

Only Nomusa was not surprised when Mdingi stood up and walked out into the open space. Facing his people, he began to sing in a clear strong voice:

"High in the hills roams the mighty elephant,
lord of the forest;
The trees quiver as he passes, and the earth
trembles under his terrible feet."

His father looked astonished as Mdingi went on, telling of the preparations for the elephant hunt, the great care the chief took for the safety of his men. A teller of tales was greatly to be admired, and Zitu had not realized that his son possessed such talents.

All the people listened eagerly, and Nomusa's heart swelled with pride in her brother. How thrilling it was to hear the story told so eloquently! Everyone was tense with excitement as Mdingi sang of Sihkulumi,

"the hunter with eyes like an eagle,"

who had first seen the wounded elephant in the gathering dusk. Knowing no fear, the hunter had leaped

forward. But the vengeful elephant had only feigned
death, and attacked the hunter.

Then came the heroic climax, and Mdingi did it
full justice in his song. When he finished, the people
cheered the singer loudly. They shouted, *"Hau! Hau!"*
for their brave and kind leader. Yo! It was a day long
to be remembered.

Mdingi stood beside Zitu, and his father's hand rested on the boy's shoulder affectionately. Zitu beckoned to Nomusa.

"Come, my little hunter!" he said. "I think perhaps it was you who brought such good luck to all of us!"

Nomusa's face flushed with pride and embarrassment as she listened to her father's praise.She was glad when she could slip back among the others.

Now Damasi stood beside her, smiling. "Is this not a wonderful celebration?" he asked.

Nomusa agreed it was indeed.

"I see Mdingi is wearing a new leopard skin," Damasi went on, softly. "And Kangata has a necklace of elephant hair. Did you keep anything for yourself?"

Nomusa shook her head. "I do not need anything. After all, I had the hunt."

"Perhaps you will find new trophies on next year's hunt," suggested Damasi.

"Oh, I shall not go next year!" Nomusa said. "Next year Mdingi will go."

Damasi looked at her keenly. "Perhaps that is best," he admitted. "But I don't think Mdingi will bring back a greater story, no matter how many hunts he goes on."

"Oh, it *was* wonderful!" Nomusa cried. "It is true that nothing could be more exciting than that elephant hunt."

The fire was dying down, but its flames still illumined Nomusa's small, dark, eager face. Damasi looked at her in silence. He was thinking that life would always be interesting and exciting to Nomusa.